ARNOLD SCHWARZENEGGER

LAST ACTION HERO™

COLUMBIA PICTURES
PRESENTS

A STEVE ROTH/OAK PRODUCTION A FILM BY JOHN McTIERNAN

STARRING **ARNOLD SCHWARZENEGGER**

"LAST ACTION HERO"™

CHARLES DANCE   INTRODUCING AUSTIN O'BRIEN

CO-PRODUCED BY ROBERT E. RELYEA · NEAL NORDLINGER
MUSIC BY MICHAEL KAMEN
EXECUTIVE PRODUCER ARNOLD SCHWARZENEGGER STORY BY ZAK PENN & ADAM LEFF
SCREENPLAY BY SHANE BLACK & DAVID ARNOTT
PRODUCED BY STEVE ROTH AND JOHN McTIERNAN DIRECTED BY JOHN McTIERNAN

A COLUMBIA PICTURES RELEASE
COPYRIGHT © 1993 BY COLUMBIA PICTURES INDUSTRIES, INC

LAST ACTION HERO™

A novel by Robert Tine
based upon the motion picture.
Story by Zak Penn & Adam Leff
Screenplay by Shane Black & David Arnott

BERKLEY BOOKS, NEW YORK

Certain incidents are based on
Richard Prather's *The Meandering Corpse*.

LAST ACTION HERO™

A Berkley Book / published by arrangement with
Columbia Pictures Industries, Inc.

PRINTING HISTORY
Berkley edition / June 1993

All rights reserved.
Copyright © 1993 by Columbia Pictures Industries, Inc.
This book may not be reproduced in whole or in part,
by mimeograph or any other means, without permission.
For information address: The Berkley Publishing Group,
200 Madison Avenue, New York, New York 10016.

ISBN: 0-425-14015-6

A BERKLEY BOOK ® TM 757,375
Berkley Books are published by The Berkley Publishing Group,
200 Madison Avenue, New York, New York 10016.
The name "BERKLEY" and the "B" logo
are trademarks belonging to Berkley Publishing Corporation.

PRINTED IN THE UNITED STATES OF AMERICA

10 9 8 7 6 5 4 3 2 1

PROLOGUE

It was, thought Lieutenant Dekker, LAPD, a hell of a way to spend Christmas.

He was not what you would call a sentimental man—far from it, in fact—but the idea of Christmas being besmirched by a lunatic holding a bunch of school kids hostage was not, to his mind, in keeping with the spirit of the holidays.

The school—a low, two-story red brick building—had been surrounded by a hundred police cars for a couple of hours now, while the psychopath within, known by the unlovely sobriquet "The Ripper," kept the two hundred heavily armed men at bay. He taunted and shrieked from inside, cackling at the hostage rescue negotiators who tried various schemes to get him to give up—or, if that failed, to let at least one of his captives go.

But The Ripper, while crazy, was no fool. He knew that as long as he had the kids, he had

1

the upper hand. The Los Angeles Police Department could deploy a fleet carrier group around the school, but there was no way they would risk using it—as long as there was a chance of harming a single seventh grader.

All of this annoyed Lieutenant Dekker no end. He was a tough man, built like a truck—a big, *black* truck—and despite the relative dapperness of his lieutenant's gray suit, he looked like a mean street cop, the kind of man who not only ate nails for breakfast but enjoyed them in the bargain.

As if things weren't bad enough, there was a rumor going around that the police chief *and* the governor were on their way to the scene. Just what he needed. The lieutenant governor and the mayor were already around there somewhere. He hoped that the politicians didn't think that they were going to be allowed to meddle in something that was serious police business.

As far as Lieutenant Dekker was concerned, *he* was in charge, in total and complete control of all the forces on the scene, from Special Weapons to Emergency Medical, each poised to go into action—and nothing was happening. There were sniper teams scattered throughout the scene and a hundred cops—ordinary uniforms and the military-style units in serious Kevlar body armor—milled around their superior officer. Police cruisers blocked all access to the site, the lamps on each of them flashing red and blue in the cold night air.

Dekker shivered inside his trench coat. "Helluva way to spend Christmas," he said, aloud this time.

"Lieutenant?" said one of the uniforms standing a few feet away.

"Nothing," said Dekker. "Go check the perimeter. Secure the sidewalks. Make sure no one—and I mean *no one*—gets in or out."

"Yessir! Right away, sir!" The cop jumped to carry out the order. The perimeter was already as tight as it could be, but when Dekker issued a command you didn't hang around to debate it with him.

Dekker paced a few steps, angry and frustrated with the inaction. There was nothing he could do but wait—and hope that one of the police sharpshooters could get into a position good enough for a clear kill shot.

"Goddammit!" he growled to no one in particular. "I hate this. When I get my hands on that maniac, I'll . . ."

In that second, a rip of automatic weapons fire blasted off the roof like a hot wind. The policemen surrounding their superior would have to wait to find out what nasty fate would befall the Ripper at the chief's hands.

The gunfire shredded a line of police cars, glass scattering in the air like shrapnel. Suddenly, dozens of men were dropping to the asphalt, covering up, sheltering from the deadly hail of bullets.

There was silence for a moment, the o

3

sound being the gentle tinkle of shattered glass falling to the ground. Then:

"Ho! Ho! Ho!" The Ripper's voice was high and unsteady. You didn't have to be a head-shrinker to figure that this guy was seriously deranged. "Hey, pigs! I got a present for you!"

A long-barreled sniper's rifle came sailing off the roof of the school and clattered on the street. A moment later something larger and heavier was hefted out of the darkness. It was the lifeless body of the lead SWAT marksman. The corpse tumbled off the building and fell on the roof of a parked police cruiser, the body thwacking the thin metal panel with a sickening thud.

Dekker, still crouched by the side of the vehicle, stared at the cadaver for a moment, his eyes wild with hate and anger. "Sonovabitch!"

The Ripper's voice blew out of the darkness. "I warned you! No cute stuff!" He paused a moment, as if choosing his words with great care. "Now, bring me my helicopter—or I start throwing out kids next! Got it?"

Dekker's face was contorted with rage. "Let the children go!" he bellowed. "Goddamn you, Ripper!"

But The Ripper was silent, as if feeling that he had already stated his case as succinctly as possible.

The cop stepped up to Dekker, having completed his hurried security inspection.

"The perimeter is secure, sir. An armored division couldn't get through it."

Dekker nodded grimly. "Good." At least something had been done right.

But the bad-natured lieutenant was wrong. There was one way into the crime scene, and Jack Slater had found it. Powerfully, relentlessly, LA's toughest cop strode forward, his forceful steps crunching on the path that led directly to danger.

But Slater didn't have a foot on the ground. As he ground inexorably forward, his boots dented and buckled roof after roof of the police cars barring the way to the school. He was wading through a sea of flashing light like a juggernaut, like a football player driving for the goal line.

Appearances, in Sergeant Jack Slater's case, were not deceiving. He looked and dressed as tough as he really was. He was a six-and-a-half-foot mountain of a man, his shoulders as broad and as hard as a car bumper.

He was dressed in a torn T-shirt, a well-worn bomber jacket and old blue jeans. The heavy boots on his feet looked as if they gave him the traction of a tractor. Completing the ensemble was a handful of Rugar Blackhawk, a forty-four, a fist of blue-black metal—the largest and most powerful handgun in production and, in the right hands, a weapon of terrifying, deadly high performance.

The most peculiar thing about Sergeant Ja

Slater—his heavy Austrian accent—had never been remarked on by anyone who knew him.

Slater wore a three-day stubble of beard on his chin. Pasted in his mouth was a well-chewed cigar. You didn't have to look too closely to figure out that Sergeant Jack Slater was in a very, very, *very* bad mood tonight. The mixture of maniacs and school kids was calculated to produce a foul humor in a man not noted for lightness of temperament.

He stepped from the hood of the last police car, heading for the barricades, never breaking stride, walking by Lieutenant Dekker as if his superior officer weren't even there. Not even the lieutenant's famous evil glare managed to slow the determined cop down.

"Don't even think of it, Slater," Dekker barked. "You hear me? You're gonna put that artillery away and wait for the hostage negotiation guys to get something going. Got it?"

Slater ignored him, walking straight for the school, his eyes fixed forward, like a marine on drill parade.

There was nothing Dekker could do but trot along beside his insubordinate subordinate. "Goddammit, Jack, I am *talking* to you. The last time you pulled this shit, people lost body parts!"

But Slater walked on, his eyes locked on the darkened school buildings.

Dekker stopped. "If you go in there, Slater, I'm warning you, it means your badge."

This time, Slater showed a sign that he had

been listening to his superior officer. Without breaking stride, the cop dug in the pocket of his jeans and pulled out his badge. He tossed it over his shoulder at Dekker. A silent, but eloquent, resignation.

The next line of obstacles stepped into his path. Two extremely well-dressed men—too well groomed to be poorly paid policemen—tried to stop him.

Slater's voice was low and threatening, even though his words were relatively reasonable. "It would be best for everybody if you got out of my way."

One of the men managed a sickly, slightly ingratiating smile. Both walked backward as Slater barreled forward.

"Jack—I know as mayor of this great metropolis, you and I have had the occassional little tiff . . ."

This was something of an understatement. The last time Jack Slater and the mayor had had a "tiff," the mayor had threatened to make sure that Jack Slater never again saw daylight as a free man.

". . . But you see," continued the mayor, "my colleague here is the lieutenant governor . . . he flew down from Sacramento to personally monitor the situation."

The lieutenant governor stepped up and started to speak, sounding determined. "Slater—here's what I think. The—"

Slater didn't care what the lieutenant governor thought and he let him know as concisely as possible. He reared back and socked him squarely on the chin. The man's eyes snapped shut, and he toppled to the ground, out cold.

"Slater!" yelped the mayor.

"When the governor gets here, call me," he said, marching toward the school building.

The last line of defense was a lone, strong SWAT-team cop stationed at the base of the stairs that led to the roof of the elementary school. He was crouched there, gun in one hand, his walkie-talkie in the other. The squawk box crackled to life.

"Carter!" The voice was Dekker's. "You there?"

"Yes, Lieutenant."

"Slater is attempting to enter the building. Do not let him in. Repeat. *Do not let him in.*"

The SWAT cop nodded at the handset, as if Dekker could see him. "Roger, Chief. Piece of cake."

Just then, Slater tapped him on the shoulder. Carter whipped around and faced him.

"Hey," said Slater. "You want to be a farmer?"

"A farmer?"

"Yeah," he said. "Here are two achers." Sergeant Jack Slater kicked the man hard in the crotch. The force of the blow, and the sheer white-hot pain, propelled the hapless SWAT cop three feet into the air. The walkie-talkie went flying one way, the gun the other.

8

Slater caught the walkie-talkie on the fly and spoke into it. "Dekker," he said ominously. "The next one—I'll hurt." Then he crushed the handset, splintering the plastic case as if it were nothing more than a nutshell.

It was on the stairs that Slater discovered the first signs of The Ripper's savagery. Bodies were strewn on the steps—adults, men and women, teachers Slater figured, who looked as if they had been felled by a murderous, bloody wind. He hardly glanced at the ragged, horrible wounds—they were run-of-the-mill in Slater's line of work—and he wasn't shocked by the barbaric nature of these sudden deaths. The only effect the corpses had on him was to make him all the more eager for the coming confrontation. He checked the clip in his weapon and smiled to himself. He was looking forward to this.

The door to the school roof blasted off its hinges, and Jack Slater stood there, gun in hand, his face grim and dark—he looked like a judgment from a vengeful and unforgiving god. He seemed to tremble slightly in his anger. His eyes swept the scene.

Cowering in a corner, huddled together, were a crowd of fifth graders, their eyes wide with terror and their cheeks stained with tears. Most shrunk back at Slater's arrival, afraid that yet another maniac had shown up, to do them more harm. But a few allowed themselves a little hope—they knew what the Good Guys looked like these days.

Slater fixed on his nemesis, The Ripper. He was presiding over his hostages, his eyes gleaming evilly. The psychopath was dressed in the uniform of a lineman for the telephone company—right down to the yellow plastic hard hat—and he was holding a fire axe.

The uniform told Slater how The Ripper had gained access to the school, and the axe revealed how the victims on the stairs had met their gory deaths. But there was a problem with that axe. Not that Slater had any doubts that he could take on any axe-wielding maniac fate cared to throw in his path; the problem with this axe was that the blade was held against a little boy's throat. A little boy Jack Slater knew very well.

"Dad . . . ," said the kid. "Help me."

"Yes," said The Ripper. "Daddy's come to help his little boy at long last." The Ripper spoke with a speech impediment, a sinister sibilant lisp. It was the one thing he was known to be sensitive about—you did not get on The Ripper's good side by making fun of his defect. "Jack Slater . . . What kept you? Your little Andy here has been getting worried . . ." He pressed the sharp blade of the weapon a little harder against the boy's throat.

"I promised him you'd come . . . I gave him my word of honor he could watch you die." The Riper dropped his air of exaggerated concern and mannerliness, the look on his face turning cold and stony. "The gun. Get rid of it."

Slater's face had betrayed no emotion whatsoever. He spoke very calmly. "Has he hurt you, Andrew?" he asked.

Terrified though he was, the boy managed to shake his head weakly from side to side.

"Nawww," said The Ripper. "I wouldn't hurt my little pal. But you hurt me, didn't you, Jackie boy—*you put me in a cage.* Put me in a cage and threw away the key for ten long years. I don't forget things like that, Jackie."

"You should have gotten the death penalty."

The Ripper grinned. "You're absolutely right. I should have gotten the death penalty. Except your illegal search rendered the blood-stained axe inadmissible as evidence. Remember? So I cheat the hangman, go away for a while and come back. Which brings us to this little scene. Neat, isn't it? I guess you could say *you* brought this on yourself, Jack." The grin vanished. "I said, lose the gun."

Slater hesitated a moment and then let the heavy weapon drop from his hand. "All right. I'm unarmed. Now let the boy go."

The Ripper shook his head slowly. "Jackie, Jackie . . . what do you take me for? I know you better than that. *One weapon?* Jack, who are you kidding?"

Slater shrugged. It was a slim chance, but it was worth a try. He yanked up his T-shirt, pulled out the three guns nestled in his waistband and dropped them one at a time to the hard gravel roof. "Okay?"

"C'mon," The Ripper urged. "You know that's not all of them. The knife, Jack. The knife."

"What knife?"

The Ripper rolled his eyes. "C'mon, Jack. Don't play dumb with me. You know which knife. The one you always have taped to your calf."

"Oh. That knife." Slater knelt down, tore the dagger off his skin and tossed it at The Ripper's feet.

"Is that all, sport?"

Slater nodded. "Yup. That about does it, except for, well . . ." Slater started patting down the pockets of his leather jacket as if looking for his car keys or his wallet. "Unless you call *this* a weapon."

He fished a grenade out of the jacket. Nonchalantly, he pulled the pin and dropped the bomb right in front of The Ripper.

"There," said Slater. "*Now* I'm clean."

The Ripper's eyes flicked down to the grenade, then back to Slater. Then he grinned sarcastically.

"Brilliant, Slater. Just brilliant. I guess I have to surrender."

Jack Slater shrugged. "That's a live grenade."

The Ripper shook his head. "No, it isn't. You wouldn't kill your own son."

"Looks like we're all dead anyway," Slater observed.

"Well, let's see . . ." The Ripper loosened his grip on the kid slightly. "Andy . . . pick up the grenade. Have a close look, why don't you?"

Still quaking with fear, Andy knelt and picked up the grenade, showing it to The Ripper.

"I see . . ." The Ripper nodded. "It's a fairly convincing fake, Slater—but it's still a fake. Your toy can't hurt the kid." He brandished the axe menacingly. "But my toy can."

It was true that the grenade could not explode, but Andy proved that it could still do some damage. The boy pressed a stud on the top of the bomb, and a three-inch blade shot out of the side. Without a moment of hesitation, Andy planted the knife in The Ripper's thigh.

They could hear The Ripper's shriek of pain two blocks away. Slater dove for one of his guns, and Andy made a break for it. The Ripper launched the axe at Slater, the heavy blade whooshing by, just an inch from Slater's scalp.

Then five things happened at once: The Ripper grabbed the boy by the arm and yanked the knife from his own leg. Slater raised his big gun and fired, just as The Ripper plunged the blade straight at Andy's heart.

Then a sixth thing happened: the entire scene went out of focus.

ONE

The action did not stop. You could still hear the sounds of shouts and screams, loud gunshots and pounding music. The problem was that you just couldn't make out what was going on.

"Focus!" shouted Danny Madigan. He had seen the movie at least a dozen times before, and he knew that this was the best action sequence in the film.

"C'mon, Nick, get it in focus," Danny muttered, squirming in his seat. He looked around, peering through the gloom at the few other patrons, eight or ten people slumped in the torn-up seats of the Pandora Theater. None seemed to have noticed that the climax of *Jack Slater III* had gone off the cinematic rails.

Danny cupped his hands around his mouth. "Come on, Nick! *Focus!*"

The groggy wino in the seat behind Danny's stirred and opened a single bloodshot eye.

"Hey," he croaked, "where are your manners, kid? People are trying to get some sleep here."

Danny scrambled out of his seat and raced up the aisle of the theater.

The Pandora had been built in the thirties, and had been, in its day, one of the great New York movie palaces. You could still see, high up in the eaves, the elaborate, dusty Moorish moldings and statuary that had been all the rage in movie theater design sixty years earlier.

But the old place had fallen on hard times. As the neighborhood declined, so had the fortunes of the Pandora. It had gone from being a first-run house to being an old, second-string theater that served primarily as an all-night flophouse for Times Square derelicts.

It was Danny's home away from home too—but with two big differences. One was that *he,* unlike the other patrons, came for the movies. The other was that he was not an aging, alcoholic, almost-destitute homeless man.

Danny Madigan was a bright-eyed eleven-year-old boy, beset with all the hopes and fears that his age entailed. Right then, fears seemed to outweigh hopes; with the onset of puberty he was aware that there was something strange going on in his body. He was also scared most of the time—not scared of anything in particular, just the big wide world in general—and felt thin and puny, friendless and poor.

On the plus side, Danny Madigan loved action movies, Jack Slater vehicles in particular.

They made sense to him in a way that the rest of the world did not. He could trust them completely: Jack Slater kept his word. Jack Slater was always right. For Jack Slater the impossible was merely routine. If you messed with Jack Slater, you ended up wishing you hadn't.

Danny raced across the lobby of the theater, the ticket-taking popcorn seller hardly stirring in his slumbers as the boy dashed for the staircase that led to the projection booth. Danny spent so much time at the Pandora that he pretty much had the run of the place.

Things were much as he expected in the cramped projection room. The two mammoth projectors were pointed at the screen like artillery pieces, the great reels turning slowly. Between them, in his chair, was Nick, the projectionist, slumped forward, his eyes closed. He was snoring slightly.

"Nick? Nick? Are you okay?"

Nick awoke with a snort and blinked, as if not quite sure where he was. Then he slid his glasses back up his nose and peered at Danny.

"What? What happened?"

"The climax of the movie. It's on the fritz."

Nick jumped a little, as if he had gotten an electrical shock. He looked out of the peephole at the screen, then made a quick adjustment to the projector, bringing the movie back into focus.

If any of the men slumped in the seats downstairs had been interested in the crowning action sequence of *Jack Slater III,* then they would have been disappointed. By the time Nick fixed the film, the movie was over and the credits were rolling. If one of the winos wanted to know how the feature ended, he would have to sit through it all over again—the movie, conveniently, ran continuously all day long.

"I never used to do that," said Nick sheepishly, embarrassed that Danny had caught him asleep on the job.

"It's okay. I've seen this Slater six times. I just got worried. I wanted to make sure you were all right."

"Still," said Nick. "It shouldn't have happened."

Nick had been a movie projectionist for most of his long life, and it was a job he took very seriously. Sixty years separated Nick and Danny, but they had several strong bonds in common. Both were, deep down, gentle, easygoing souls. And both seemed slightly at sea in the world, the older man just as bewildered at the close of his life as Danny was at the beginning of his. And both loved movies with the same unrelenting, unshakable passion.

Nick had another great obsession. For as long as he could remember, ever since childhood, Nick had been captivated by magic and magicians. Pasted all over the walls of the projection booth were old, yellowing posters of famous magicians, a veritable sorcerer's Hall of Fame. There was the Great Thurston, Merlin

Junior, Harry Blackstone, Corky Withers and, in the center of the portrait gallery, the greatest of them all: Harry Houdini.

Nick could spend hours telling stories about the great magicians of the past, but right then, he was more interested in Danny.

"Are *you* okay?"

"Yeah . . ."

"What's the matter with your hand?"

Danny smiled ruefully and rubbed the raw scrape on his knuckles. "Aww, it's nothing . . ."

"You get in another fight?"

Danny shrugged. "I'm just so tired of getting robbed. I feel like I'm always walking around with a big 'please mug me' sign on my back."

Nick smiled. "It's just a phase."

"A phase? Fine. But why do I have the feeling that I'm the only one going through it?"

"You're not the only one, Danny. It'll pass. Trust me."

"I hope so."

"I can make you smile . . ." said Nick slyly.

"You can? That would be some trick."

"The new Jack Slater is opening at the Odyssey on Friday."

Danny shrugged. "Oh, like I didn't know that . . ." He deepened his voice and did his best to sound like a movie announcer. He had memorized the commercial for the new movie weeks ago. "'They killed his second cousin—*big* mistake. *Jack Slater IV*.'"

"Well," said Nick with a studied indifference.

"I have to check the print tonight. Midnight. Just me." He casually examined his finger-nails. "I can arrange for you to gain admittance, if that kind of thing has any interest for you."

Danny's eyes grew wide. "Are you serious? See Jack Slater IV before it opens? Who do I have to kill?"

Nick laughed. "No one." He glanced at his watch. "Get to school now—if you hurry, you'll only be four hours late."

"Yeah," said Danny. "I guess . . ."

Danny made his way down from the projection booth, stopping in the lobby long enough to examine, for the umpteenth time, the carboard cutout advertising *Jack Slater IV* in the foyer.

It was larger than life size, an eight-foot display showing Jack Slater looking his toughest. In one hand he had a giant assault rifle. Clutched in the other fist was a stick of dynamite, fuse lit. The trademark cigar was between his teeth.

Clinging to him, as if sheltering in the lee of his powerful body, was a beautiful girl. She was a blond and blue-eyed sixteen-year-old, the most gorgeous girl Danny had ever seen in his life. Stenciled across her chest were the words AND INTRODUCING MEREDITH CAPRICE.

Danny stared at the girl longingly and then sighed, heading for the door of the theater. Out on the street, in the glare of broad daylight, he blinked and felt let down at having left the make-believe world behind. In the cold sunlight, the world did not look like a particularly welcoming place, especially in the grungy strip of New York City he was in now.

Even at mid-morning, Forty-Second Street, west of Broadway, was a nasty place, peopled by a motley collection of shifty-eyed drug dealers, living-dead junkies and scary-looking prostitutes, their exact gender not immediately apparent.

He paused a minute and looked back at the Pandora. The old building seemed to sag on its foundations, its paint flaking. The ornate facade seemed to be mocked by the tawdry peep shows and topless bars that were the theater's neighbors. She was like a once grand old lady fallen on hard times.

Across the street was a vacant lot and a huge sign decorated with a construction company logo: COMING SOON—MANN'S MULTIPLEX 18 WITH SONY IMAX AND RIDE-SHOW THEATER. The present was difficult enough, but Danny had the feeling that for the Pandora the future would be filled with fresh indignities.

TWO

Class was well under way by the time Danny slipped into his place. No one had noticed that he was absent that morning, and no one noticed now that he had finally shown up. No one asked for an excuse, a late slip, or a pass. Discipline was not the strong suit of PS 131. Danny sighed. He might as well not be here for all anyone cared.

The English teacher, Mr. Donaldson, did manage to work up a fair amount of enthusiasm for his subject—Shakespeare's *Hamlet*—but he was having trouble translating his excitement to his bored class. As he paced back and forth in front of the video monitor on the desk, he had fallen back on the old teaching trick of trying to make Shakespeare's plays "relevant" to a bunch of seen-it-all inner-city junior high school kids.

"Ghosts!" he exclaimed. "Sword fights! Sex! And everybody dies! Shakespeare's *Hamlet* couldn't be more exciting." Thirty pairs of heavy-lidded eyes stared at him. No one looked convinced by Mr. Donaldson's zeal.

But he wasn't quite ready to give up yet. "You see, despite his inability to act, Hamlet is still an inspiration. You might call him one of the first action heroes."

Danny's antennae went up. Action? In Shakespeare? It sounded far-fetched, but Danny was open-minded enough to give it a shot. The rest of the class did not seem to be buying it, though. All over the room, yawns were being stifled.

The teacher saw that he was in danger of boring his class into a coma. It's a rule in contemporary English instruction that you never try to teach a book that has not been made into a movie. It was time to hit his class with a video.

"But I think you'll get what I'm saying when you take a look at the movie of Hamlet. So why don't we just roll it?"

He snapped off the lights and turned on the VCR.

It was the classic 1948 Laurence Olivier version of *Hamlet,* slow, stately costume drama—and in black and white. As soon as they saw this novel feature, two or three kids passed out like narcoleptics.

From the back of the room, Mr. Donaldson spoke. "People considered Olivier the greatest actor who ever lived. Some of you might have seen him as Zeus in *Clash of the Titans.*"

The scene was Claudius kneeling in the gloomy chapel of Elsinore Castle, hunched before the altar, examining his hands as if they were literally stained with the blood of Hamlet's father.

"What if this cursed hand were thicker than itself with brother's blood? Is there not rain enough in the sweet heavens to wash it white as snow?"

A young Laurence Olivier appeared on the screen in full Hamlet getup, stealing furtively into the shadowy room. Danny knew enough about the play to be aware that Hamlet had a major beef with Claudius, and it was obvious that the Prince of Denmark had his enemy right where he wanted him. Danny was caught up in the story, wondering what Hamlet would do next.

Hamlet studied the figure before the altar. "Now I might do it pat," he whispered, "now 'e is a prayin', and so he goes to heaven. And so I am revenged."

Yeah, thought Danny. *So what?*

"A villain kills my father, and for that, I, his sole son, do the same villain send to heaven . . ."

"Don't talk," Danny whispered. "*Do it.*" He stared at the screen hard, as if willing the hesitant prince to action.

Olivier stalked the length of the chapel, bearing down on the still-praying Claudius. But Hamlet appeared to have changed somewhat. He was still dressed all in black, his princely medallion was still hanging around his neck—but his back and shoulders were huge, bulging out of his dark costume.

Wait a minute, thought Danny, *I know those shoulders.*

Laurence Olivier was gone. Jack Slater had taken his place. And he looked mighty annoyed. Danny felt the tingle of anticipation shoot through his entire body. Things were about to start happening—big time. Danny glanced around the room. His fellow students were half or wholly asleep. Even Mr. Donaldson stared blank-eyed at the screen, as if failing to register the sudden and exciting changes in Hamlet.

"Claudius," intoned Jack Slater. "You killed my father." For once, the Austrian accent came in handy and seemed to help you believe he was playing a Danish character.

The movie wasn't a movie anymore. It was a series of coming attractions, sort of "Hamlet's Greatest Hits." Out of nowhere the deep-voiced announcer from a movie trailer kicked in. "Something is rotten in the state of Denmark . . ."

Slater reached down and grabbed a handful of Claudius's robe. He yanked the man to his feet, raised him high above his shoulders.

"Big mistake," growled Jack Slater. He hurled the King of Denmark through the stained-glass window, colored shards of glass exploding like hard fire.

"And Hamlet is taking out the trash," bellowed the announcer.

Shakespeare had never been so much fun. Or so noisy. The Jack Slater theme was blasting out of the tinny speakers of the video monitor.

As far as Danny knew, weapons in Shakespeare's play were pretty much limited to swords and spears and the occasional bodkin, but Slater wasn't satisfied with that. He was on the rampage now, thundering through the desolate stone halls of Elsinore Castle, an Uzi in each hand, spitting hot lead at guards who were at a disadvantage being armed only with lances.

But Slater did give a nod to tradition. The scene shifted rapidly. Jack was brooding in the graveyard, Yorick's skull in his hand.

"Alas, poor Yorick. I knew him well . . ." But their friendship in the past didn't stop him from using his old pal's remains as a weapon. Suddenly Slater wheeled and fired the skull like a fastball, the teeth embedding in the forehead of a guard.

"Heads up," said Slater.

They smashed back to the castle. Slater yanked aside a curtain to reveal old Polonius.

"Stay thy hand, fair Prince," he said. "The lovely Ophelia is even now our captive. Should you exact thy vengeance, the maiden shall unto you be delivered, portion by bloody portion."

This did not please Jack Slater. He leveled his Uzi and blew the guy away. "Who said I'm fair?"

"No one's gonna tell this sweet prince good night," the announcer intoned.

Slater stood in front of Elsinore, a cigar clamped between his teeth. "To be or not to be?"

He pulled a bundle of dynamite from his robes and lit the fuse with the cigar. Then he tossed the explosives over the castle wall.

"*Not* to be," Slater decided. The castle erupted in smoke and flame.

And then it was over. As Elsinore disappeared, Shakespeare's Hamlet, the *real* Hamlet, returned. Danny sighed. He knew that Hamlet was a masterpiece—he knew this because he had been told it a million times—but Jack Slater was so much more *fun*.

On the screen, Olivier was speaking. "Roasted in wrath and fire, and thus o'er-sized with coagulate gore, with eyes like carbuncles, the hellish Pyrrhus old grandsire Priam seeks."

It sounded promising, but Danny had a feeling it wasn't going to lead anywhere . . .

THREE

Danny was relieved to get out of school—he always was—but home wasn't all that much fun either. He shared a cramped one-bedroom apartment with his mother—she got the bedroom; he had to sleep on a fold-out couch in the living room—because there wasn't much money around since his father died. But at least at home he could escape, he didn't have to worry about taunts and teasings from classmates. Once home, Danny could watch TV and try to forget about his generally lousy day.

Irene Madigan took over the job of worrying once the school day was done. She worried about money and the future, but most of all she worried about her son, his progress in school, his isolation, his lack of friends.

She was getting ready for work while he watched TV, her waitress uniform unzipped and open down her back.

"Danny, zip me up," she said.

"Sure." Danny stirred from the couch and fastened the back of his mother's dress. "There you go. Anything else?"

"Yes. Regale me with your life story starting with 8:30 A.M. today, first-period American History, and make it good. Something heroic, like along the lines of 'Ma, I cut class so I could donate a kidney.'"

"You know?" said Danny, his spirits sinking.

"I know. The school called."

"And I thought no one cared."

"Someone cares. *I* care. Were you at the movies again? You were, weren't you? And that crazy old man is an accessory."

"Nick's not crazy!" Danny protested.

Irene Madigan sank down on the couch, out of gas.

Danny was silent. He hated letting his mother down. Her life was hard enough without her having to worry about him on top of everything else. "Mom, I'm sorry . . ."

"I know it was hard coming here," she said grimly, "leaving your friends behind and all. But what was I going to do in Green Castle, Pennsylvania, after your father died? Pick green beans at fifty cents an hour? I didn't plan it, Danny. I didn't *plan* to be a widow at forty."

"I know that," said Danny bleakly.

Irene smiled at her son and draped her arms across his shoulders. "Hug me." Danny squeezed back. "I'm sorry, Mom. I won't cut class again."

"Let me hear the 'P' word."

Danny smiled. "Promise."

"Good." She smoothed his hair. "Listen, I have got to work double shifts this week. Dinner and graveyard."

"When I get a little older, I'll be able to do that too," said Danny.

Irene Madigan shook her head. "Not while I'm around, kiddo—I'm looking at a college man."

"College?" College was at least five years in the future—light-years away.

"That's right. But before that, I have Friday night off. Maybe me and you and your friends could hit a flick."

"My *friends*! What friends?" Friends seemed even more remote than a college education.

"Okay, just the two of us then, We'll go out and see a good foreign film, like *The Seventh Seal*."

This, to Danny's way of thinking, was a truly lousy idea. He didn't mind the thought of going out with his mother—it was her choice of entertainment. "Mom, I like *action* movies."

Mrs. Madigan had stood and was fixing her hair, staring at herself in a mirror. "So? This one has Death in it. He wears a big hood."

Danny jumped to his feet. "A big hood! My God, let's go now!"

Irene Madigan refused to give up. "I'm telling you, you'd like this movie—it's got people kicking off all over the place."

Danny looked skeptical. "Yeah? I heard he sits around and plays chess."

"So? Between slaughters he relaxes a little." She straightened her uniform and grabbed for her purse.

Danny laughed. "Nice try, Mom. Keep it up. You might convince me in a year or two."

"I've got to run." She kissed her son lightly on the forehead and then dashed for the door. Danny settled down to do his homework, the TV blaring.

Around ten-thirty, he knew it was time for him to go to bed. But who would know if he didn't? In less than two hours, Nick would begin rolling *Jack Slater IV*. Danny could see the blackness, the empty theater, Nick nodding off at his post, the film unspooling unappreciated in the dark.

Danny shook his head as if trying to clear the vision from his mind and tried to concentrate on the last bit of homework. That lasted almost five seconds. He closed the book with a snap, hesitated a moment, then jumped to his feet, jammed his keys in his pocket and headed out of the apartment.

Danny opened the door a crack, saw that someone was coming down the hall and quickly stepped back inside. He waited a moment for the corridor to clear, then slipped out and put his key in the lock.

Then someone hit him from behind, bashing him back into the apartment and pinning him against the wall. The sound of the switchblade was as loud as a gunshot. Danny managed to shoot a quick look over his shoulder. The mugger was about eighteen, with bad skin and bad teeth and eyes the color of flint.

"Tell me a lie, I take an eye. You alone?"

Danny nodded, frightened to death. "Yeah."

"Okay," the punk ordered, "the bathroom. Move it. Now."

He shoved Danny across the apartment and into the tiny bathroom, pushing him to the tile floor. Then he tossed him a pair of handcuffs.

"Do yourself to the drain," he commanded.

"You . . . you gonna rob us?"

"Ohh, now *there's* an idea," the punk said sarcastically. "Chump."

Danny's fingers trembled as he slipped a handcuff over his wrist. Part of him was terrified and humiliated. But *all* of him was filled with rage. His features were contorted with anger, the fury showed plainly on his face.

The punk smirked at him. "Hey, don't get so upset. I didn't realize I was in the ring with such a tough guy." He tossed the switchblade lightly in his hands and then placed it on the edge of the bathroom sink.

"There you go, sport. Your move."

Danny looked from the guy's face to the knife and hesitated. With all his being, he wanted to reach out and grab the blade and drive this guy out of his house. But he could not bring himself to act.

"I'll make it easier for you," the punk said

tauntingly. Very slowly he turned his back. "Take your shot."

Danny was torn. He wanted to be brave, but he couldn't be. It was risky. It was stupid. Tears of frustration welled up in his eyes.

The punk turned back, smiling evilly and retrieving the knife. "You'll never forget that. As long as you live. Now lock yourself up."

Danny sat on the bathroom floor, miserable, listening while the apartment and his mother's meager possessions were ransacked. He was so wretched that had he died in that moment he probably would not have cared.

He jumped when the mugger stormed back into the bathroom. The smirk had been replaced with a snarl of rage.

"What the hell is it with you?" he demanded. "You got junk! No jewelry! No VCR! No cash. Nothing! Nothing but a shit TV that'll get me ten bucks! Shit!"

"Sorry," said Danny in a small voice. Instantly, he hated himself for apologizing for not having anything worth stealing.

"Sorry? Sorry ain't good enough." For a long and terrible moment Danny thought the guy was going to hit him hard or cut him with the knife.

But instead of hurting him, the mugger did something much worse. He humiliated him.

He tossed the key into the bowl of the toilet. "Go fish, amigo."

The instant the front door slammed, Danny hobbled to the toilet. With his free hand he groped around in the water for the key, tears streaming down his face. He felt pathetic and pitiful, a weak runt.

Jack Slater would never allow this to happen to *him*.

FOUR

FOUR

It was a slow night for crime in the 87th Police Precinct, so it didn't take the usual three-to-four hours to process Danny's crime report. Still, it took over an hour, allowing Danny plenty of time to examine his surroundings.

The muster room was a study in gloom. Four or five banged-up desks stood out in the middle of the room, islands of messy paperwork. An elderly clerk was slumped at one of them and seemed barely to be alive. He was typing with one finger, pausing for a full five minutes after each character, or so it seemed to Danny.

The detective taking Danny's report didn't seem much more efficient, but he had filled out all the forms required, given him some mug books to look at and called Mrs. Madigan at work to assure her that there was no reason for alarm.

Danny squirmed in his hard seat, darting

anxious looks at the wall clock. It was almost midnight.

"Remember now," the detective said, "your mother says you have to go straight home. She'll be there the minute the shift is over."

"Yessir." Danny dug something out of his pocket. "Do you need this?"

"What is it?"

"Its the key for the handcuffs that the guy . . . you know, the ones he used on me."

"Oh."

"You know, like evidence or something."

"No. It's okay. You keep it."

Danny had the distinct impression that the New York City Police Department did not exactly consider what had befallen him that evening the crime of the century.

"Can you get home okay?" the detective asked, as if hoping that he wasn't going to have to arrange transport for the kid. He too had noticed that it was almost midnight—the end of his long shift.

"I'll be fine."

"Good. You ever been mugged before?"

Danny nodded.

The detective sighed heavily. "My kids have too. It's the world we live in these days, I'm afraid. If we find the guy, we'll give you a call."

Danny knew how the world worked. "But you're not going to find him, are you?"

The cop couldn't meet his eyes. "We do what we can," he said. Which meant "no."

"I better get going," said Danny.

"Take care . . ."

It was raining outside, and the dark, almost empty streets around Times Square seemed scarier than when they were thronged with people. Homeless men in cardboard bunkers slept on heating and subway grates, and other, more frightening figures lurked in the shadows and alleyways. One by one the marquees of the theaters on Forty-Second Street went dark. Soon, the city that never slept would be dozing.

Danny knew he should go straight home, but the thought of returning to the ransacked, empty apartment depressed him. His spririts needed the lift of the familiar—the darkness of the Pandora and the comforting mayhem of *Jack Slater IV*.

The Pandora looked shabbier in the damp darkness than it had in daylight. More run-down, if that were possible, and forlorn than Danny had ever seen it before. Soaked to the skin, Danny tried the front door and found it locked.

"We're closed," snapped the girl in the ticket booth. She was counting up the meager takings and was not happy to see Danny.

"I'm looking for Nick," Danny called through the thick, scuffed glass.

"Try the side door," she said, shaking her head in disgust. Nick was just a crazy old movie-mad coot as far as she was concerned.

Danny raced down the alley flanking the

theater, sprinted up the rickety cast-iron fire escape and pounded as hard as he could on the dented fire door.

"Please, Nick," he whispered. If Nick had started the movie and retreated to the projection booth, he would never hear Danny's knocking.

Then, to his relief, the door swung open. "I about gave up on you," said Nick.

Danny stepped in out of the rain and shook himself like a wet spaniel. "I'm sorry."

"So?" said Nick with a grin. "How do I look?"

Danny's eyes swept over Nick. "I've never seen anything like it," he said tactfully.

Nick was dressed in a threadbare old uniform, a movie usher's getup that probably dated from the day the Pandora had opened its doors. It was a faded red with brass buttons and gold piping on the seams and legs. The outfit was completed with white gloves, white spats and a round paging-Philip-Morris pillbox hat. It was also *very* snug on Nick—so tight that Danny figured if Nick drew a deep breath, brass buttons would start ricocheting around the room like live rounds.

"Not too tight?" Plainly, he thought he looked terrific and wanted compliments.

"Not at all. Besides, that's the style these days, isn't it?"

Nick's eyes were bright with excitement. "I *always* wanted to be a magician, except I had these tiny hands." He held his white gloved hands out for inspection. Danny had never noticed it before, but Nick's hands *were* kind of small for a man. "But I still knew it was show business for me. My first job? Ushering right here in the Pandora, back when it was a vaudeville house."

Nick's chest swelled with pride, testing the threads that secured his buttons to the material of the uniform.

"That was just the beginning. Less than twenty years later, I was off the floor and in the booth. The best projectionist in New York City."

"That's great Nick," said Danny, "it really is." He was touched that the old man considered his less-than-meteoric rise in the entertainment industry a fitting accomplishment in life. "Let's get started."

But Nick barred his way. "Wait. Aren't we forgetting something?"

Danny looked confused. "We are?"

"Of course."

"What?"

"A ticket, Danny. You got to have a ticket to see a movie, don't you?"

Danny's heart sunk. "But the ticket booth just closed." And given the demeanor of the girl in the kiosk, he doubted that he would be able to get her to open it again.

Nick shook his head. "Not an ordinary ticket. A special private screening requires a special ticket. And I have just the one."

With a grand magician's flourish and some clumsy sleight of hand, he produced a ticket.

But the old man was right. This was no ordinary ticket. It was bigger than a normal pass and far more ornate. This one was gold and silver and seemed to shimmer slightly in Nick's gloved hands.

Danny gaped. It was like nothing else he had ever seen before in his life. "What . . . ? What is that thing?"

A note of awe crept into Nick's voice; he was hushed and reverential with wonder. "Harry Houdini himself gave me that, Danny. I was your age, and my pop, he took me backstage after a show."

"Really?"

Nick nodded. "And he made a gesture, Mr. Houdini did—and *this* was in his hand, and he whispered to me . . ." Nick leaned closer and hissed. "'This is a magic ticket,' he said. 'The greatest magician in India gave it to me and the greatest magician in Tibet gave it to him. It's a passport to another world. It was mine,' Mr. Houdini said, 'and now it's yours.'" Nick stopped whispering. "And now, Danny, it's yours."

"Mine?" Danny took the ticket in his hands and turned it over, examining it closely. "What does it do?"

Nick looked embarrassed for a moment. "I'm not really sure. I never had the courage to use it."

He smiled sadly. "I kept it all these years, and I wanted to try it out—but I was so afraid it wouldn't work. You see, Harry Houdini was like a god to me—what if he was faking? I couldn't stand it."

"Wow," said Danny.

"He said one other thing . . ."

"What did he say?"

"He said, 'This ticket has a mind of its own, young man. It does what *it* wants to do.'"

"What does that mean?"

Nick shook his head slowly. "I don't know. But it always made me a little edgy."

Danny grinned mischievously. "Well, there's only one way to find out, right?"

Nick nodded, a gleam appearing suddenly in his aged eyes. He took the ticket, held his breath for a moment and tore it. For a split second there was something—a spark, a flash, a microsecond of glimmering golden light. Maybe it was a trick of the light, maybe they both imagined it and it was gone as quickly as it had come, but somehow both Nick and Danny had the same sudden feeling: that the ticket had been triggered.

Nick dropped one stub into an old-fashioned ticket barrel and handed the other half to Danny.

"Please retain your stub."

"You bet." He thrust the ticket into the breast pocket of his shirt and forgot all about it.

Danny was in heaven. He was seated dead center of the empty movie palace, a tub of fresh popcorn on his lap. Nick's voice boomed out of the public address system.

"Shall we see if Mr. Slater wins this time?"

"Jack Slater can't lose," Danny shouted. "Never has. Never will."

And with that, the houselights began to dim . . .

FIVE

The camera rushed in low over the dark blue of the California Pacific, straight at the cliffs of the coastline. Spread out along the bluffs was a series of big houses, each mansion sitting among wide, lush lawns and gardens, green cordons sanitaires separating each estate from the others. You paid a lot for privacy in the high-rent district.

The largest house on the cliff was a rambling gabled mansion that mixed a number of architectural styles—English country house, Southern plantation, Greek temple, but with Spanish colonial predominating—making for an end result that was more impressive for its pretension than its splendor. It was also the most expensive house in the area, as well as being the most secluded.

This suited the owner just fine. In fact it was the isolation of the estate that had attracted Antonio "Tony" Vivaldi more than the fabulous view, the giant swimming pool, the perfect lawn tennis courts or any other of the luxurious features of the vast estate. As the leader of the biggest collection of gangsters in Southern California, Tony Vivaldi liked to keep his doings pretty much to himself, away from the prying eyes of strangers and the sophisticated surveillance techniques of half a dozen law enforcement agencies.

Tony's business methods were, to put it mildly, a little unorthodox, particularly when "discussing" business with people who had interests that ran counter to his own. As the movie opened, Tony was engaged in doing just this.

Tony Vivaldi was a tall, heavy, powerful-looking man, his skin the color of olive oil. The clothes he wore were expensive, if not in the best of taste, and on his fat fingers he wore not one, but two pinkie rings, each with a diamond the size of a walnut. They glittered in the bright sunlight, and the beams got in the eyes of the hapless man strung up and hanging from one of the stately trees on Tony's enormous front lawn.

Tony strode back and forth in front of the very scared guy, shaking his head and clicking his tongue.

"Frankie, Frankie, Frankie . . . why you keep on with the insults?" Although he had never set foot in Italy, Tony spoke with a pronounced Chico Marx–type accent.

Hence: *"Frankie, Frankie, Frankie . . . why-a you-a keeponwit-a da insults?"*

Tony Vivaldi was tough and as street smart as they came, although he had had little formal education. He had never gotten beyond kindergarten (at the age of five he had announced, in the middle of "Eentsy-Weentsy Spider," that *"play dough is for saps. I want da real dough"* and dropped out).

The gangster had learned reading on the *Daily Racing Form* and arithmetic from the numbers racket and derived much of his personal style from Salozzo the Turk in *The Godfather*. (A sensitive man, he still got all choked up during the scene where Salozzo got plugged in the middle of a plate of veal at Louis's Restaurant in the Bronx.)

In short, Tony Vivaldi was the type of character who got the Italian American Defamation League all hot and bothered and yelling about Leonardo da Vinci, Michelagelo, Galileo and Lee Iacocca when he appeared on the silver screen.

He also had a taste for violence, torture and terror that put him in the front rank of movie psychopaths, along with Hannibal Lechter (*"da guy gotta bad rap"*), Freddy Krueger (*"how can I meet dat guy?"*) and Pinhead (*"nice look"*).

Nailed to the tree, level with Frankie's face, was a small round target. Tony touched it as if it were a talisman.

"So tell me, Frankie. How come always with the insults?"

Frankie was more scared than he had ever been before in his entire life. "I would never, ever insult you, Mr. Vivaldi," he said quickly. "You gotta believe me."

Vivaldi glowered at his trussed captive. "When you lie, Frankie, that's an insult—I know you Jack Slater's favorite second cousin in the world . . ."

Back in the real world, Danny crammed a handful of popcorn into his mouth. Although he was *in* the real world, right then he was so caught up in the movie that he had a certain amount of trouble distinguishing between fact and fiction. The rough days at school, his lack of friends, what his mom had to go through every day, even the humiliation at the hands of the muggers had been washed away in the drama unfolding on the screen.

Jack Slater's favorite second cousin in the hands of evil Tony Vivaldi! Danny had seen this scene unfold so many times—the Ku Klux Klan got hold of Slater's Uncle Zeke, the Shining Path guerillas snatched Slater's best friend, the Khmer Rouge kidnapped Slater's Aunt Sylvia—that he knew exactly what was going to happen.

"You're gonna be *sorrrry,*" he said aloud, exhaling little bits of popcorn onto the back of the seat in front of him.

Tony was oblivious to the warning. "So," he said, "you tell me does he know that my mob and the Torelli mob have signed a secret pact to control all the drugs in Southern California?"

Danny nodded to himself. There it was. The major plot revelation right on schedule.

"No! No! No!" protested Frankie. "He don't know nothing about dat." (The Vivaldi manner of speaking was nothing if not contagious.)

Vivaldi did that clicking thing with his tongue again, which was really quite scary. "Then, what do you talk about then?" (*Den, whatta you talk-a about den?*)

"Uh . . . Uh . . . I guess we mostly talk about muzzle velocities. You know?"

"What's that?" (*Wha'zat?*)

Frankie wriggled a little. "Well, muzzle velocities . . . That's, ah, that's a gun thing. It refers to the speed at which a bullet leaves a gun barrel."

"Not fast enough!" said Tony decisively. Then: "Guns," he said, nodding to himself. "I like guns. I like guns a lot."

"Who doesn't?" said Frankie.

Tony Vivaldi smiled. "You know who *really* likes guns?"

"No." Frankie was not sure he wanted to hear the answer to that question.

"My friend. My friend Mr. Benedict."

Frankie did not think this sounded good. Whoever Mr. Benedict was Frankie was not sure he wanted to meet him. However, he had little choice in the matter.

Vivaldi snapped his fingers. In that same second, a shot rang out and the target nailed to the tree next to Frankie's face vanished. Frankie jumped, his eyes bugging out, a scream rising from his throat.

Fifty yards away, on the very edge of the wide patio of the house, a man sat at a table and had just interrupted his breakfast to illustrate Tony Vivaldi's little speech. He put the gun down next to his plate and returned to his grapefruit. Mr. Benedict was a very distinguished executioner, one of the finest practitioners of this particular trade, which made him much in demand with people like Vivaldi.

Benedict was tall and blond, and two of his features stood out. His lips were thin and cruel, and he had a habit of pursing them right before he killed you. The other thing that people noticed about his face was his eye—his left eye, to be exact. It was artificial, and this morning it had a bull's-eye target on the surface where the pupil should have been. Nonchalantly, he popped the orb out of his head and polished it on the sleeve of his silk shirt.

Vivaldi giggled when he saw him do that. "Meet Mr. Benedict, Frankie. The guy is the genuine article, you better believe it. Sometimes he likes to bake while he's shooting people."

"B-bake?" said Frankie.

"That's right." The gangster chuckled at the recollection. "This other time, I seen him putting together a spinach lasagna, alla while he's shootin' the kneecaps of these union guys. Then he makes them taste the lasagna! Can you believe that?" Vivaldi chuckled a little more. "What I'm saying, Frankie, is that Benedict can take you out—easy as cake."

Benedict muttered under his breath. "That's easy as *pie,* you Sicilian schmuck."

"Mr. Benedict is a great shot, Frankie. But he can do more than kill you. He can let you live five minutes or fifty before you die—the man is a surgeon. Now, you want for me to have him operate on you?"

Frankie was frantic, near tears. "I *swear* to you. I don't know anything."

Vivaldi was *so* sad about the outcome of his little talk with Frankie. "Have it your way." He trotted the length of the veranda to Benedict.

"Dump him at his place," he ordered the assassin. "Let him live a couple of minutes . . . He bought it. He actually believes that me and Old Man Torelli are getting together. Beauty part is, nobody's gonna know different. Not till the funeral. Then *everybody* knows."

Vivaldi's evil smile filled the screen. "You're gonna pay," whispered Danny. "Oh, are you gonna pay . . ."

The police cruiser rolled to a halt in front of a modest but pleasant-looking two-story house in the eleven hundred block of Angelina Street. Both cops in the car looked at the neat little residence, the well-tended garden and the trimmed lawn and then exchanged a look.

"What do you think?" asked one.

His partner checked the address on the charge sheet. "We got the right place." Both men got out of the car and approached the front door warily, guns drawn.

"You sure this is the right number? It sure doesn't look like a crack house to me." They were at the front door, and it was the first time either of them had encountered a drug den that had a welcome mat and a bird feeder.

"What do you want? Sixty guys dancing on the lawn throwing cocaine at each other? Kick the door in."

But before they had the chance to beat their way into the house, they were interrupted by the squeal of brakes as a 1966 Bonneville convertible roared up to the house. The car screeched to a halt at the curb.

Danny was on the edge of his seat. It was time for the man himself.

The dented door of the Bonneville swung open, and Jack Slater hauled himself out. But something was wrong. He had no weapons. Instead of cradling a carbine or his big Ruger street canon, he had two bags of groceries.

"Hey, guys," he said to the cops. "What's up?"

"Quiet, Slater! This is a drug bust."

"Drug bust?" said Slater. "My second cousin Frank lives there."

"*Your* second cousin?"

"The only drugs you're gonna find in there are aspirin, and if you touch that door, you're gonna need them."

Now the two cops were really confused.

"Look," said one, "maybe there's been a mistake. We got an anonymous tip."

Jack Slater pounded hard on the front door. "Frank? Frank?" There was no reply. "That's strange. He's usually home by now."

He put the groceries down and then reared back to kick the door in. At the last moment, he remembered whose door he was kicking in and caught himself. He turned the doorknob and led the way into the house.

Second Cousin Frank was tied to a chair placed right in the middle of the living room. You couldn't miss him.

He was in much worse shape than he had been when Danny had seen him last. His face and chest were bloodstained. His eyes were glazed and his breathing forced and shallow.

"Frank! Frank! What happened?"

With his dying breath, Frank managed to gasp out his last words. "Jack . . . Tony Vivaldi and the Torelli mob are joining forces," he said. Then he died.

Anger was beginning to build in Slater. "Someone will pay for this," he announced to the two cops.

"Look," said one, pointing to the corpse. "There's a note."

Pinned to Frank's shirt was an envelope with Slater's name neatly printed on it. Jack grabbed it and tore it open. Inside were a series of three-by-five cards. The first one read: 5. The second: 4.

Puzzled, Slater flipped to the next one: 3. Then he got it.

"Bomb!" he announced and dove for the front door.

Nine point nine minutes into the movie came the first explosion—and it was a gratifyingly big one. The entire house was incinerated, a pleasing tower of fire and debris climbing into the sky. All down the street, windows blew in and cars flipped over.

Danny made his prediction: "Slater's okay. Minor wound. Both cops dead."

Slater dusted himself off, ignoring the bloody gash in his forearm. The other two cops were hanging in the scorched branches of the palm tree on what had once been Frank's front lawn.

"Like I said," declared Danny.

But Danny's forecast hadn't been exactly accurate—one of the cops wasn't quite dead yet. He was alive just enough to manage to croak out the words "Two days . . . to retirement . . ."

Slater's face had turned to stone. He turned and marched to his car. Oddly enough, the Bonneville didn't have a scratch on it.

SIX

The little suburban Hiroshima that Danny
had witnessed was just the beginning, an over-
ture, a pyrotechnic prelude to the first big
action sequence of the movie. As if on cue, a big,
powerful pickup truck came roaring down the
formerly peaceful street, the brawny engine
roaring, the tires squealing as they laid down a
track of rubber on the asphalt.

There were five thugs in the vehicle, two up
front, three in the bed of the truck. As befit
villains in a Jack Slater movie, each man was a
strapping bruiser, most of them decorated with
facial hair, scars and tattoos. To a man, they
were decked out in what the well-dressed thug
was wearing: jeans, leather jackets, very dark
sunglasses. And they were armed to the teeth.

But there were *only* five of them. Danny had
seen Slater duel with twice as many thugs at
once, and he had hardly broken a sweat. The
upcoming encounter was obviously just a

warm-up for the real mayhem that would occur later in the movie.

Slater vaulted into the Bonneville, the engine bursting into life the instant he hit the seat. The car peeled out, tires smoking, the engine wailing. Slater drove one-handed—the other was occupied with the big Ruger Blackhawk.

The chase was on. One of the thugs in the pickup grabbed a bundle of dynamite sticks from the bed of the truck, lit the fuse and heaved it at Slater.

Jack down-shifted and swerved, the explosives bouncing on the trunk and flying high in the air. They detonated like an artillery shell, in a cloud of black smoke and orange flame.

Danny was in ecstasy. There was nothing that got his blood pumping harder than a good, rubber-burning, dynamite-throwing, engine-racing car chase.

The action on the screen was also having an effect on the ticket stub that peeped over the top of Danny's pocket. As if it were absorbing the mayhem in the chase, the ticket was glowing, pulsing with soft gold light. Danny was too caught up in the chaos unfolding in the movie to notice.

Another sheaf of dynamite was lofted into the air, tumbling end over end, the fuse crackling. Slater raised his weapon and fired, a thundering report that seemed to fill up the theater. The shot nicked the edge of the bundle, altering the trajectory of the explosives, deflecting them away from Slater.

They seemed to be coming straight at Danny, his eyes growing bigger and bigger as the deadly bundle bust through the screen and fell with a thump in the aisle of the Pandora Theater.

Danny stared hard, watching as the dynamite came rolling back down the aisle, bouncing like a terminal tumbleweed.

"Uh . . . Nick . . . ? Hello . . . ?"

But Danny was marooned in the middle of the theater, cut off from Nick by the all-encompassing sound of the gunfire, the explosions and the screaming engines on the screen.

Danny wasn't sure why he did what he did next. He slammed his popcorn tub over the dynamite, the way you might trap a mouse. Inside the container, he could hear the fuse continuing to crackle and pop. The dynamite was trapped, but all that stood between Danny and oblivion was a thin sheet of oily cardboard. Not enough protection, he decided.

"Now that," he said, "was smart."

In an instant, Danny was on his feet and running, bolting down the aisle as fast as he could go. But it was too little, too late. He hadn't gone ten yards when the explosives detonated. Danny felt a strong, hot wind sweep over him, and his feet left the floor, blowing him into the air. The world went pure white, and the theater spun away, fading in a roiling storm of noise and bright shining light.

So this is what it's like to die, Danny thought. *Pretty scary.* In those seconds, his whole life passed in front of his eyes—twice—and was just starting on its third rerun when everything changed again.

The gut-wrenching battle on the screen got louder and louder, as if the movie were coming back to life, opening up and swallowing Danny whole. He also felt as if he were being pulled back to earth.

Then he landed—whump!—hard, but not so hard that he couldn't make out some of what was going on. He was sprawled on his back, looking straight up at the sky. That was good. Danny had the distinct feeling that he had been jolted back to reality—sort of.

There was warm wind in his face, not the dynamite kind, but the genuine, midsummer article, and there were trees going by overhead. But there was something wrong . . . Unless he was very much mistaken, until a few minutes ago, he had been seated in a movie theater. A movie theater in New York City—where it was a rainy, cold October night. This was definitely day. And warm.

Suddenly, Jack Slater's giant gun appeared above his head and blasted three times, firing beyond him. The trio of loud booms brought Danny back to earth with a crash. He yelped and hugged the seat, eyes closed tight, pushing his face into the vinyl.

Slater was just as amazed as Danny. "Who are you?"

Danny opened one eye. "Don't shoot me. I'm Danny Madigan. I'm a kid."

"How did you get here?"

"I'm not quite sure where 'here' is, sir, but I don't think you want to know."

The pickup was bearing down on them now, the guy in the passenger seat leaning out the window, his big fist stuffed with a gun.

"Stay flat," Slater ordered. "Close your eyes. Don't move."

Danny was anxious to be helpful. "Would you like me to shut up too?"

"That would be nice."

Two big slugs tore into the body of the Bonneville, the force of impact rocking the big car on its springs. Slater floored the gas pedal, and the vehicle leapt forward. Bullets were zipping and whinning in the air, and the car zig-zagged and swerved to avoid the fusillade.

But instead of just running away, Slater was determined to fight back. He swiveled in his seat and raised the huge Ruger Blackhawk in both hands. He sighted down the barrel, taking precise, deadly aim.

Danny peeked at him. "You're driving with no hands," he said in amazement.

"You think it's easy? You should try it some-time."

"No, sir," said Danny quickly. "I was just kind of wondering if it was safe."

"You have to practice a lot—and never do it in heavy traffic."

"Never," said Danny emphatically.

One of the goons was standing up in the bed of the pickup truck, leaning back, just about to let fly with another dose of dynamite. Slater fired. A split second later, the slug slapped into the guy, throwing him out of the truck and through the windshield of an ice cream truck parked on the side of the road. There was a moment of delay, and then the dynamite detonated, a staggering blast that blew the truck to smithereens and showered a half block with a deluge of frozen treats, zipping through the air like cold shrapnel.

Another tough guy went down, felled by a lethal blow to the neck from a frozen Nutty Buddy drumstick ice-cream cone. Slater saw the thug topple and smiled grimly.

"What do you know? Iced that one," he muttered. "To cone a phrase."

That was all Danny needed to put it all together. His eyes grew wide, and he sat bolt upright in the seat, oblivious to the bullets that were perforating the air around the car.

"Oh my God, that voice, the bad puns . . . it's *him*." He blinked several times very quickly. "Wait a minute . . . How did I get . . ." He swallowed heavily. "Oh boy . . ."

The Bonneville rocketed around a corner, and the landscape changed abruptly.

So much had happened in the last few minutes, Danny was having trouble taking it all in. He gaped at the streets. Gone were the neat suburban houses with their well-trimmed lawns, and in their place were the drab streets of some sort of downtown, a light commercial zone.

"Hey, we were just in the suburbs. What happened?"

Danny quickly lost interest in the landscape. Yet another dynamite bundle had sailed into the car and landed with a thump on the floor. He was hypnotized by the fuse fast burning down to the explosives.

"This is not happening," Danny chanted. "Repeat. This is not happening." He allowed himself to peek. The fuse was about a quarter of an inch away from the dynamite. This definitely, undeniably, indisputably *was* happening. And if that dynamite detonated, then it would be the last thing that ever happened to Danny Madigan in his brief life.

Casually, Slater reached down and pinched off the fuse between his finger and thumb, as if snuffing out the dynamite were nothing more dangerous than extinguishing a candle.

As soon as that danger was averted, a new one presented itself. The car was screaming down a narrow side alley, straight at a lumbering tanker truck that was backing out into the tight thoroughfare. There was not enough room for them to get by, and to hit the gas truck meant a very fiery end.

Slater read the situation perfectly. There wasn't enough room for a *whole* car, but with a little fancy driving, there would be room for *half* a car. He took a deep breath and yanked the wheel sharply to the right. Just as expected, the car popped up on two wheels, ignoring gravity, and skated by the tanker.

An instant later, the Bonneville dropped back onto all fours and raced away, plunging straight into the alley. And into a dead end. The brick wall that closed off the passageway seemed to be getting closer at an alarming rate. There was no way out.

"Boy," muttered Slater, "does this really suck weenie or what?"

He jammed on all the brakes and threw the car into a smoking one-hundred-and-eighty-degree turn. The Bonneville careened to a shuddering stop, inches from the dead end, facing back the way it had come.

Danny was pale green and sickly looking. He wiped his mouth with his sleeve, a picture of misery. "I booted. Sorry," he said. Then he added in his own defense, "I thought for sure I was going to die."

Slater was staring ahead, straight down the alley. "Sorry to disappoint you," he said, his eyes narrowing. "But you're going to live to enjoy all the glorious fruits life has to offer: shaving, acne, premature ejaculation."

The pickup truck full of thugs was at the mouth of the alley. The last two goons in the back of the truck hopped out of the bed, dropping to the street, Czech MP-5 machine pistols cradled in their arms. Both men were grinning.

It was all beginning to make sense to Danny: the wild action, the impossible stunts, the sudden shift of landscape. "Hey . . . I know why they're smiling—this is a movie set. That's how the scenery changed."

Slater took his eyes off the pickup long enough to shoot a weird, uncomprehending look at his unexpected passenger. Then he returned to the business at hand. He stared ahead, his eyes cold and lifeless, they were the eyes of a predator, a shark in his natural habitat. He pressed the accelerator, revving the powerful engine. At the far end of the alley, the pickup revved back. The two vehicles faced each other like angry bulls.

"You're going to play chicken, aren't you?" said Danny excitedly. "Just like Jack Slater."

"Fasten your seat belt, please. Do you have fingers?"

"Fingers? Yeah." Danny held up both hands. "I've got ten of 'em."

"Good. Cross as many of them as you can . . ." Slater stood on the gas, and the big car bucked forward. At the same moment, the pickup started rocketing down the alley. The noise of two potent engines filled the air as the automobiles cooked rubber, hurtling toward each other.

The Bonneville and the pickup were flying toward each other, each driver hunched over his wheel, each intent on the immediate annihilation of the other.

For a second, it seemed to Danny that neither driver's nerve would break. Then he remembered: *he was in a movie!* Of course the bad guy would swerve—and a split second later, he did just that.

The pickup clipped the Bonneville and caromed up onto a pile of wooden cargo pallets. This being a movie, the heap of debris was, of course, stacked in steps—in other words, ramp shaped. And sure enough, right on cue, the truck charged up the stack and went airborne, heading straight for the rear wall of a building. The pickup was doing sixty when it smacked through the bricks, and at the instant of impact, the truck burst into a ball of flame. The two guys in the cab of the truck toppled to the ground, both of them burning merrily. One managed to stagger to his feet and totter through the alley.

Two thugs remained. The fiery demise of their comrades did not seem to have deterred them from the task at hand: exterminating Jack Slater. They raked the Pontiac with withering machine gun fire, blowing out the windows and shredding the body work under a torrent of hot lead.

Jack Slater looked as if he had had just about enough of these guys. He grabbed the bundle of dynamite from the floor of the car, cadged a light from the thug on fire and tossed the explosives at the last two, uninjured, goons.

The blast blew the guys off their feet and threw them through an upper-story window of the building that backed onto the alley. Glass rained down, but not a shard touched Slater or the awestruck Danny.

Jack Slater lit a cigar. "Just a couple of second-story men."

Almost in a trance, Danny swallowed hard.

"I'm in the movie," he whispered, his head awhirl. "Holy shit, I'm actually *in* the movie . . ."

Dumbstruck, he pulled the ticket from his shirt pocket. It was still glowing, more faintly than before, but definitely still radiant.

"Nick—Houdini—he wasn't faking." Danny couldn't wait to tell his old friend. It was great being in a movie, and he would have a lot to tell Nick. *If* he could find a way *out* of the movie.

SEVEN

The police station wasn't a bit like the one Danny had visited earlier that—evening? day?—he wasn't really sure. The real one, the one in New York, had been decidedly low tech, a grungy hovel furnished in classic American Civil Service. This one, the one in the movie, was way too clean, and it was suffused with cool blue-lit movie smoke that seemed to come from nowhere. It was also packed with people.

The booking desk was a study in chaos as every kind of lowlife—hookers, pimps, dealers—all talked at once. Cops were pushing their collars through the crowd. Angry citizens shouted complaints at the desk sergeant. Every phone in the place seemed to be ringing.

Slater waded through the roiling crowd and seemed to be more or less oblivious to the anarchy. Danny, however, gaped, hanging back to take in all the entertaining turmoil.

Slater stopped. "What are you looking at?"

"I was just in a real police station, and this one is much nicer."

"*Real* police station? How do you mean, *real* police station?"

Danny gave Slater a sly, knowing look. "You know, as opposed to a movie police station."

Jack grabbed Danny by the collar of his jacket and lifted him off his feet, hauling him into the detective's squad room, carrying him like an angler with a trophy fish.

"Movie?" he growled. "What movie?"

"Jack!" shouted one of the detectives. "Your ex-wife on line two."

"Great. All I need." He plunked Danny down in a hard chair next to his desk. "You," he said, pointing as if at a recalcitrant puppy dog. "Stay."

Slater slung himself behind his desk and punched line two on his telephone. He tried to inject a smile into his surely voice.

"Sweetheart, how are you? Uh-huh . . . yeah . . . yeah . . . uh-huh." As he spoke, he scrabbled in a desk drawer, looking for something buried deep in the clutter.

Danny continued to stare around him, quite taken with the police station. It was just like every cop movie he had ever seen, right down to the tried and true cinematic cliché of "odd couple" partners.

The watch commander sat behind his desk assigning diverse colleagues without a hint of irony. "Oiler!" the cop shouted. "You're partnered up with Waterman."

Oiler was a fat pig of a man with all the accoutrements of slobdom. Waterman, of course, was a prim, neat, handsome woman.

"Kraus! You're teamed up with Rabbi." Kraus, needless to say, was a tall, blond, strapping Aryan type. Rabbi was, well, a rabbi.

Danny smiled and nodded to himself. "Some things are just classics. They never go out of style."

Slater was still on the phone. "Uh-huh . . . yeah . . . that's right . . . yeah . . ." There were half a dozen cassette tapes in the desk drawer, each of them labeled: "Creditors," "Internal Affairs." Slater selected one tagged "The Shrew." He popped the tape into the player on his desk top, hit play, and then laid the phone down next to the speaker.

The tape rolled. "Yeah? How much money? Uh-huh?"

Relieved of the duty of talking on the phone, Slater got up from the desk to get himself a cup of coffee.

"How do you get to Carnegie Hall?" shouted a man coming into the squad room.

Slater whipped around. "Practice!"

The two men obviously were old friends, and they shook hands warmly. The newcomer was dressed in the conservative gray suit, crisp white shirt and boring tie that, in the movies, said: FBI.

"John Practice, you old SOB! What are you doing away from Washington?"

Danny gawked, not just because he was

seeing Jack Slater smile for the first time, but because the guy he called John Practice was F. Murray Abraham, the guy from the movies *Amadeus* and *Scarface*.

The FBI man lowered his voice conspiratorially. "The bureau thinks something strange is going on between—this is top secret—"

Slater interrupted. "Tony Vivaldi's mob is joining forces with the Torellis."

Practice shook his head in wonderment. "How the hell did you know that? You are amazing! Look, I'll catch you later. I have to call DC."

Danny waited until Practice was out of earshot, then he whispered to Slater.

"Better watch it. That guy killed Mozart."

Slater's smile was gone. "In a movie, right?"

Danny nodded vigorously. "That's right. *Amadeus*. It won eight Oscars."

"Oscar who?"

"Oscar who?!" Danny yelped. It was true that the Academy of Motion Picture Arts and Sciences had never given the Jack Slater movies the respect they deserved, but he didn't think that Jack Slater would ignore them altogether.

"Look, I saved John Practice's life in 'Nam, so I'll be sure to be on the lookout—*now, no more movies.*"

But the action-movie clichés were still coming thick and fast. That instant, the glass door on the far side of the room swung open with a crash and there stood the big, black chief of detectives, Lieutenant Dekker.

"Slater!" Dekker seemed to be quivering with rage. This was not unusual for him—when the lieutenant was calm, he was never less than apoplectic. When he was *really* angry, he was eye-popping, veins-in-the-neck-bulging enraged. Danny smiled when he saw his old pal from *Jack . Slater II*.

"Hey, Lieutenant," said Slater. "How you doing?"

"In my office! Now!"

Danny wondered if by any chance this was going to be the scene in which the older, higher-up-the-chain-of-command cop gives a chewing out to the younger, unconventional-and-very-violent cop.

"Goddammit, Slater!" growled Dekker. "I got the city council chewin' my eggs off for that plane you crashed!"

It *is*, Danny thought happily. Slater stood stoically, impassively taking his boss's heat.

"I got the mayor scheduling parades up my Lincoln tunnel for that stunt you pulled down at the beach! Everyone is lining up for a chance to dingle my berries, and it's all because of you!"

Slater was as still as a statue. "Just doing the job."

This did not strike Dekker as a reasonable defense. "Doing your job! Do you call doing your job smashing up half the cars in the department? Do you—"

Danny turned away from the harangue for a moment—the tirade was quite entertaining, but the watch commander was still handing out assignments, and they were even more interesting.

"Ratcliff," he shouted. "You're pulling duty with the Animated Cat."

Ratcliff was an attractive woman. The Animated Cat was . . . a cartoon character, about four feet tall and furry. Danny's jaw dropped, and he looked around to see if anyone else thought this was as strange as he did. But no one had so much as raised an eyebrow.

Dekker continued chewing out Slater. Slater continued to just stand there and take it.

"You've given this department the worse reputation in the country! I've got the Chamber of Commerce doing cartwheels in my cocoa factory, and I have the American Civil Liberties Union white water rafting in my fudge river canyon! Do I make myself clear, Slater?"

Danny couldn't keep his mouth shut for a second longer. "Wait! I can prove this is a movie."

Dekker's eyes swiveled in on the boy, like the big guns on the decks of a battleship. "Who the hell are you?"

"Look out there!" Danny pointed. "There's a cartoon cat out there."

"So?" said Jack Slater. "He was supposed to be back on duty today. He was only suspended for a month."

"A four-foot cartoon cat detective. Doesn't that kind of say 'movie' to you?"

"Kid, the department waived the height requirement years ago."

"C'mon," Danny insisted. "You're trying to tell me this is a real police station? A real police station, and an animated cat just walked in."

Slater shrugged. "And he'll do it again tomorrow. What's your point?"

"That cat is one of the best men I've got," growled Dekker. "Slater, who is this little twerp? And why is that smile on his face?"

Danny was grinning from ear to ear. "I just love the way you two fight, knowing how you really feel about each other."

Dekker folded his arms across his chest and glared hard at Danny. "Pray tell, how *do* I feel about this weird-looking sack of shit?"

"Oh, that's easy. You're dearest friends."

"We are? How do you figure that?" Dekker demanded.

"See, after your wife left you for the circus midget and Jack told everyone he drove her to New England to the diphtheric clinic, when he came back, you said, 'You saved me from public humiliation. Jack, you're my dearest friend.'"

Dekker was stunned, horrified—it was plain from the look on his face that Danny's every word had been true. "Slater," said Dekker hoarsely. "You promised me you'd never tell a soul."

Slater was just as flabbergasted as his dearest friend. "I swear I never did."

"Then how did *he* know?"

Both detectives stood over Danny, drawing

themselves up to their full height. "So," said Slater. "How did you know?"

Danny smirked. "Easy. It was all in *Jack Slater II*."

"*Jack Slater II*? What the hell is that?"

"A movie," said Danny.

EIGHT

Danny was really quite surprised—he hadn't thought two big men would move quite so fast. The instant he had made that crack about the movie, Jack Slater and Lieutenant Dekker swept him up, hustled him down the hall and threw him in an interrogation room. This had all happened in a matter of seconds, and the third degree began immediately, bright light in his eyes and everything—just like in the movies.

Dekker stood over him. "You know the good cop/bad cop routine?"

Danny nodded. "Of course."

"Only bad cops in here," Slater snarled. "Two *verrrry* bad cops."

"Who are you?" demanded Dekker.

Danny decided that, movie or not, it would be wiser to tell the truth. He rattled off his name, address and phone number, like a prisoner of war giving his name, rank and serial number.

"Danny Madigan. 855 West 40th Street. New York City. 212-555-1113."

Dekker snatched up the phone, dialed the number quickly and listened to the computer-generated voice inform him that there was no record of that number.

"No such number," he said. "No name, either."

Well, of course not, Danny wanted to say. *You can't call out of a movie into the real world. Any damn fool knows that.*

"How did you get in my car?" shouted Slater.

The truth had gotten Danny nowhere. He decided to change tactics. "Um . . . I, uh, slipped off a walk-over bridge, fell, and you saved my life."

"Truth at last," said Dekker. "Now we know about him. What about you, Slater? Why were those hard cases after you?"

"My second cousin Frank found out some crucial drug information—"

Danny couldn't resist butting in. "I wouldn't put too much faith in what Tony Vivaldi told him . . ."

Slater glowered at his small prisoner. "How do you know Frank mentioned Vivaldi?"

"I know a lot about what's going on," said Danny quickly. "If you'd just listen to me . . ."

Dekker put his hand on Danny's shoulder and smiled slowly. "Son, I've got the perfect listener for you. Slater, meet your new partner."

Now, this was just the about the most perfect

piece of movie logic Danny had ever encountered. In the real world, a kid with no known name and address would have immediately been turned over to some do-good agency to take care of him. In the movies, though, the natural thing to do was to team him up with a rough, tough cop in the middle of a dangerous drug investigation.

Danny didn't care. He beamed and his heart pounded hard. Never in his wildest dreams had he thought he would get the chance to meet Jack Slater, never mind become his odd-couple partner.

But Jack Slater looked less than thrilled. In fact, he looked sick to his stomach. "Better to die," he said.

"Now let me shuck this down to the corncob for you, Slater. Your new job is to wet-nurse this half-pint twenty-four hours a day until I say otherwise. We got to find out everything he knows."

"But—"

"No buts. Now, both of you get your sandy cracks out of here because I'm having a horrible time holding my temper."

Slater strode through the police station. Danny hurried along next to him, doing his best to keep up. He was bubbling with enthusiasm, delighted at the way things had turned out.

"You'll learn to love it, Jack—we're perfect buddy movie material."

"Again with the movies," grumbled Slater.

"I tell you—we're perfect. I'll teach you to be vulnerable, you'll teach me to be brave."

They were passing the charge desk. Danny grinned and waved at the desk sergeant. "Hi, I'm Jack Slater's new partner. Jack and I will be working together for the duration of the film."

"Film?" said the sergeant. "Jack, what film?"

"Never mind." He grabbed Danny and hurried him out of the building, storming down the steps to the street.

Danny didn't give up. "Come on, Jack, you know I'm right. In the real world, they would assign me to a social worker, not team me up with a police detective."

"This is the real world," insisted Slater.

"Okay, here's one: tell me how I know they tortured Frank and stashed him behind his front door?"

Slater stopped and stared at his new partner. His was plainly puzzled.

"Because I saw it on-screen, Jack. Because *this is a movie*."

Slater scowled. "You're very clever. But the reason I'm not roaring with laughter is because someone killed my favorite second cousin. Bi—"

"Big mistake," said Danny quickly. "Big mistake, right? That *is* what you were going to say, right? Gee, how could I have known that?"

"Nobody likes a smart ass," snapped Slater.

Danny stopped walking. "Okay. Shoot me."

"Shoot you?"

"That's right. Point your gun at my head and pull the trigger. Come on. Do it. I double dare ya."

"I wish I could."

"But you can't, can you? You're not gonna do it, are you? And you know why? Because people like you don't kill kids in movies. 'Cause, believe it or not, you're the good guy, Jack."

"You really believe you're in a movie, don't you?"

"*Yes!*"

Slater looked at his watch, then at Danny. "Okay. You have ten minutes to prove it to me. After that, I prove you wrong. My way."

"Your way? What way is that?"

"I shoot you."

NINE

The first thing Danny noticed about the video store was that the girl behind the counter was way too beautiful to be working for minimum wage in a place like that. Danny was delighted—as far as he was concerned it was further proof that he was definitely in a movie.

"Quick," he said, rushing up to the counter. "Where are your Schwarzenegger films?"

"Foreign films are in the back."

"Foreign? No, no, no. Action! The guy is an action star."

"Oh, action star. Why didn't you say so? Right over there." She pointed to a wall of video cases. Standing in front of them was a large, detailed standing cutout for *Terminator 2*. Except it wasn't Arnold Schwarzenegger in the black leather jacket, with that one red eye, his face half-machine—it was Sylvester Stallone!

Danny was stunned. "No . . . ," he gasped. "It's not possible. It can't be."

"He was fantastic," said Slater. "Absolutely. His greatest performance ever. The man is an artist."

"But . . . but that was you. *You* were in that movie."

"Please. This movie stuff is getting boring."

"You were in a movie?" said the babe at the counter. Her dark eyes were wide with wonder.

Slater had no qualms about flirting shamelessly. "Yeah, it was called *The Girl of My Dreams*. I think it starred you."

The girl blushed and giggled. "C'mon . . ."

"No, really. In fact, there was this very romantic scene where we had dinner together."

"Is this your kid?" the girl asked.

Slater shook his head quickly. "Nope. Mental patient. I have to take him downtown."

Danny was frustrated, but he hadn't given up. "What about this girl right here?" he said quickly. "She's way too attractive to be working in a video store."

Finally, Danny had something Slater could agree with. "You're absolutely right. She should be working with us. Undercover work."

The girl giggled a little more.

"Look, the point is—there are no unattractive women here."

"Nothing wrong with that."

Danny grabbed Slater by the arm and dragged him out of the video store. They stood on the sidewalk and watched the people walking by.

"Okay. Look at the women," Danny ordered.

"No problem," said Slater with a grin.

Every woman who walked by—black, white and Asian—had one thing in common: every one was gorgeous.

"You see my point," said Danny.

"No," said Slater. "I don't."

"Where are they?"

"Who?"

"The ordinary, everyday women. They don't exist because this is a movie."

"No," said Slater patiently. "This is California."

This was getting Danny nowhere fast. Luckily, Slater seemed to have forgotten his promise to shoot him. But Danny was still determined to prove to Jack Slater that he was a movie character.

"Okay, I'll tell you what—I'll take you to the house where your second cousin Frank was tortured. I can do that because I saw it. I saw it on the *screen*."

"That's ridiculous."

"Look, what did Dekker tell you? You're supposed to listen to everything I have to say, right? I mean, I know you're not big on following orders—and I admire that, really. It's part of your charm—but why not do it? Just this once."

Slather thought for a moment. "Get in the car," he said.

This being a movie and everything, Danny knew exactly which way to head to look for Vivaldi's mansion, and there wasn't even any traffic getting out of town. Even with this cinematic advantage, however, the search for the house wasn't entirely smooth. They had to cruise the coast highway for an hour before Danny recognized the neighborhood.

Slater humored him, treating his young partner as if he were an amiable, certainly not dangerous but slightly tedious lunatic. They drifted by estate after estate. Each seemed familiar, but none was quite right.

"How about that one?" said Slater, gesturing toward a mini version of the palace of Versailles off to the right of the highway.

Danny shook his head. "It can't be the one. The house we want has an ocean view. It's on the other side of the road. On the left."

Slater pointed out another house. This one was big, but not huge. "That one looks promising."

"No—I told you, we're looking for a *big* house, and I'll know it when I see it."

Slater rolled his eyes.

"Really," Danny insisted. "See, there's something you don't understand."

"So," said Slater. "Enlighten me."

Danny hauled the magic ticket out of his shirt pocket and showed it to the cop. "This ticket is magic," said Danny very seriously. "And it really works."

"Uh-huh. Of course it does—so does my decoder ring."

Danny would have to prove the worth of this ticket to Jack Slater at some point, but right then he decided he would have to start taking better care of it. Carefully, he stowed the slip in his wallet.

Then he returned to scanning the roadside. Suddenly, he pointed. "Stop—there—that's the place."

Slater immediately threw on the brakes, and the car screeched to a halt. "You sure?"

Danny examined the house closely. Then he shook his head slowly. "Nope. It's the wrong color."

"Maybe they painted the whole house overnight. Let's go investigate it anyway."

Danny frowned. "You know, you're not giving me a lot of support here. You're my partner; your job is to give me confidence."

Slater put the car in gear, and they started down the highway again. "No," he said, shaking his head. "My job is to get you out of my life as soon as possible."

"That kind of attitude is not going to get us anywhere," said Danny sourly. "It was a Spanish-style house, sort of." Then he tensed like a setter locked on a game bird. "Like that one." He pointed. "*Just* like that one."

The car rolled to a halt in front of the tall gates, and together they peered up the long driveway.

"The bad guys are in there," said Danny, his voice low and hushed, as if Vivaldi might be able to hear him.

● ● ●

Slater dug in his pocket and pulled out his badge. "I'm sorry, Danny," he said quietly, "this is for you. You deserve this more than I do."

Tentatively, touched, but unsure of himself, Danny reached out to touch the mystical badge of Jack Slater. "I don't think I've earned it."

"Earned it?" said Slater. "Of course you have."

"I have?"

"Don't you understand? You've revolutionized the entire history of police training and procedure. This is the greatest breakthrough in the annals of investigation."

"It *is*?"

"Of course. All those years I spent at the Police Academy, studying human character, learning the art of fingerprint analysis, the courses I took in hostage negotiation, the year at Harvard studying the psyche of the terrorist, that term at Oxford probing the psychology of evil—when all the time, all I had to do was point a finger and say: *the bad guys are in there.*"

Danny glared at his partner. "You think you're funny, don't you?"

"I know I am. I'm the world famous comedian Arnold Braunshweiger."

"That's Schwarzenegger," Danny snapped.

"Gesundheit."

"Very funny," said Danny as he got out of the car and started up the driveway.

Slater followed. "What the hell kind of name is that, anyhow?"

"Austrian," said Danny.

"Yeah? Well, I got you there. I was born in Newark, New Jersey. So there."

"Newark, huh? So where did you get that accent?"

Slater looked genuinely puzzled. "Vot eggsent?" he asked.

"Forget it."

The door to the mansion was an ornately carved block of solid oak. Slater hammered on the knocker, and they only had to wait a few seconds before the door swung open. They found themselves face-to-face with a very tough-looking Asian man. This was Mr. Chew, one of Vivaldi's most devoted flunkies.

He looked Danny and Slater over suspiciously. "May I help you?"

"Yes," said Slater pleasantly, "can I speak to the drug dealer of the house?"

The man blinked once. "I beg your pardon."

"It's a beautiful day," explained Slater reasonably. "And we're out killing drug dealers. We were in the neighborhood, and we were wondering if there were any drug dealers in this house that we might kill?"

Danny got the distinct feeling that Slater was not taking any of this seriously.

Neither was the butler. "I'll have to take a look inside. May I ask you to wait a moment."

"Of course," said Slater with a warm smile.

The door closed on them. Danny was tense,

edgy, tapping his foot nervously on the doorstep. "Be ready for anything," he advised Slater.

Suddenly, Slater turned and started walking away.

"Where are you going?"

Slater whirled. "I'll be back. Didn't know I was going to say that, did you?"

Danny rolled his eyes and shook his head. "That's what you *always* say."

"I do?"

"Everyone keeps waiting for you to work it in," said Danny, as if explaining something to a particularly slow child. "It's your calling card. You say it in every movie."

Slater walked slowly back to the steps. "I do? Damn."

Just then the door opened. Mr. Benedict stood there, glaring at them through extremely dark glasses. His voice was an evil and sibilant hiss.

"I understand you're interested in drug dealers," he said.

"Jack," said Danny, sotto voce, "that's him. The henchman with the glass eye. But go easy—he almost nailed Bruce Willis *and* Kevin Costner."

Slater sighed, then took a deep breath. "Sir, are you a henchman?"

Benedict shook his head. "No, I only got as far as lackey. Of course, it's all political. It's who you know. Will there be anything else?"

88

"Yeah," said Slater. "Take off your sunglasses."

Suddenly, things seemed to get serious, as if Benedict and Slater recognized each other as natural enemies.

"Who's asking?"

Slater held up his badge. "The tin man."

"Well, tin man," said Mr. Benedict, "suppose you hit the bricks."

"They're the wrong color."

Mr. Benedict raised a single eyebrow—one of those bad guy trademarks, Danny noted. "Are they? By all means, let's change them. I think the bright red of arterial blood would go nicely, don't you?"

Something made Slater and Danny turn. Facing them on the lawn was a perfect semicircle of huge, burly Rottweilers. The dogs were silent and stock-still, their eyes fixed hungrily on their prey.

Slater and Danny looked back to Benedict. "Make no mistake," he said, "these dogs obey my every whim." He snapped his fingers. The dogs formed a canine pyramid, balancing on one another's shoulders. They still hadn't taken their eyes off Slater and Danny.

"If they start tap dancing," said Slater, "make a run for it."

"Now I snap my fingers and you emerge from Rottweiler rectum sometime around noon tomorrow . . . or you take Toto and head back for Oz. Questions?"

Slater extracted a cigar from his jacket

pocket, bit the tip off and lit it. He frowned as he drew on the stogie. Up until meeting Benedict, he had thought that Danny was just some crazy kid. He still thought that—but he also knew that he didn't like this guy Benedict one little bit.

"Yeah," said Slater. "I have two questions. Why am I wasting my time on a dime-store putz . . . when I could be at home doing something dangerous like reorganizing my sock drawer?"

Benedict stiffened, his face coloring. He was used to being always the toughest guy on the block.

"And question number two: how exactly are you gonna snap your fingers . . . after I rip both your thumbs off?"

Slater had booted the tension up to the boiling point. For a moment, Danny was convinced that the two big men were going to butt heads right there on the steps of Vivaldi's mansion. The pressure was so high, the air seemed to crackle.

Then Mr. Benedict did something *really* scary. He smiled. *Then* he removed his sunglasses.

"Whoa," said Danny.

Benedict had popped the target glass eye out of his head and replaced it with another one. This one had a bright yellow happy face on it.

"Have a nice day," he hissed. He turned and started back into the house. The interview was over.

"He had one with a bull's-eye," Danny whispered to Slater as they walked back down the driveway.

Benedict stopped. Frozen in the doorway.

"And he hates his boss—called him a 'Sicilian schmuck.'"

Benedict felt as if the earth had moved. How could the kid have known that? He shot a look over his shoulder, watching the man and the boy walk away from the house. Benedict knew that they would have to meet again . . .

TEN

Tony Vivaldi was not happy. He paced back and forth in the study of his mansion, gnawing on his thumbnail as if it were a drumstick. He glared at Benedict.

"How did Slater find out?" he demanded. "I would give anything to have him join up with me—but he's so nuts, he keeps going after bad guys." Vivaldi stopped pacing and leaned over Benedict. *Where is it written I'm a bad guy?*"

Benedict shrugged. "Dunno."

"We gotta find out who talked—and him we kill, *then* Slater," Vivaldi snarled. "What's with you?"

"That kid spooks me." Benedict's voice was low and sullen. "Does this mean we change the funeral arrangements?"

Vivaldi whipped around and looked at his hit man as if he had suddenly grown two heads. "Are you outta your mind? Once Tony Vivaldi plans a bloodbath, guess what, there's a blood-bath."

"That's what people like about you," said Benedict. "You're a thoughtful host . . . I want to check out Slater's short little friend."

Slater and his short friend were miles away, in the Hollywood Hills not far from the home of Jack Slater's ex-wife. The Bonneville pulled into a parking place a few blocks away and Slater shut down the engine.

"Come on, Jack," said Danny hotly. "That guy has got to be guilty of *something*."

"The only thing he's guilty of," said Slater, "is acting like an asshole. I arrest him, I have to arrest half the population of LA. Maybe more than half."

Danny looked around. "Why did we park here?"

"In case my ex-wife is home."

"Don't worry, she's not."

"How do you know?"

"Easy. Her name wasn't in the credits."

Slater got out of the car and slammed the door so hard the vehicle rocked. "Kid, what does a doctor treat?"

"Sick people?"

"Guess again."

Danny thought for a moment. "Patients?"

Slater nodded. "Right." He held up his right arm. "Okay, now look at the elbow of my jacket. What's it doing?"

Danny looked very puzzled. "Doing? It's on your arm. It's just *there*."

"What kind of condition is it in?"

"Uh . . . wearing thin?"

"Bingo. Put 'em together and what do you get?"

"Patience wearing thin." Danny shook his head, disgusted with the lame joke. "Jeez. That was a stretch."

There was a giant four-wheel-drive Jeep parked in the driveway of the house. It was a convertible, with a thick chrome roll bar like an arch curved over the seats, crowned with a half a dozen powerful spotlights. There was a skein of bright red flames painted along the side of the jet-black bodywork.

Danny was impressed, but it was no less than he expected of Jack Slater. "Wow! Is that what you drive on weekends?"

Slater looked slightly offended. "No. That's my little girl's car."

Danny nodded approvingly. "Any girl who drove a car like that, I'd like to meet," he said.

Slater gestured toward the front door. "Go ahead. See if she's home."

"Cool." Danny stepped up and rapped on the door. A moment later, it swung open and there stood Meredith Caprice, the ingenue actress now starring in her very first role in a Jack Slater movie. In the flesh, she was just as lovely as her photograph on the standee in the lobby of the Pandora.

She had long, soft blond hair tumbling to her shoulders and wide-set innocent-looking blue eyes. The thing that interested Danny most was that Meredith was wearing a bathrobe—*only* a bathrobe, it seemed.

Things got even better. Without a word, but with a smile on her face, Meredith reached out, cupped Danny's face in her soft hand and kissed him on the lips. Danny's eyes crossed and then closed, as he surrendered himself to the kiss.

He never wanted it to end, but, to his immense sorrow, it did. Danny staggered back a foot or two, his head spinning, slightly out of breath.

"Meredith?" he said, still dazed.

"Meredith? I hope you mean Whitney."

Of course! This wasn't Meredith Caprice the actress—this was Whitney Slater, the character.

Danny did his best to recover as quickly as possible. "Yeah. Uh, sorry. Whitney. Of course."

"You're not Skeezy are you?"

"Skeezy? No. I'm . . ."

But Whitney wasn't interested anymore. She had looked beyond him to her father.

"Daddy!" she squealed and launched himself into his arms. Jack Slater's standard-issue scowl vanished, his face lighting up when he gazed at his daughter.

The two of them rocked together on the doorstep, ignoring Danny, who had to admit that this was one side of the tough movie cop that the average movie fan never got to see: Jack Slater, Family Man.

Danny trailed them into the house. It was a modest two-bedroom bungalow, but with some nice touches, like the hardwood floors and the fire crackling in the red brick fireplace.

"Hi," said Danny, trying to get between father and daughter. "I'm Danny Madigan, and I realize I haven't had that long a life yet, but I just want you to know from now on, after that kiss, I know it's got to be all downhill."

Whitney smiled her dazzling movie star smile. "Daddy, he's so cute."

Slater shook his head vigorously. "No, no, no. He is not cute. He is hopelessly insane. Pretty soon he'll start telling you he loved you in *Gone with the Wind*."

"Nope. This is her first movie."

As far as Slater was concerned, that confirmed what he had just said. "See? Now. Who's this guy Skeezy?" Like most fathers, Jack Slater had a very low opinion of his daughter's dates.

Whitney shrugged and laughed a little, a light silvery laugh that gave Danny a delicious case of the shivers.

"It's just a sorority thing," she explained. "They assign you a freshman, and when he comes to the door, you kiss him."

Danny perked up. School definitely got better as it went on. Suddenly he had a reason for wanting to fulfill his mother's desire that he go to college. He wondered if you could be a freshman for all four years . . .

"I have to get dressed," Whitney announced. "Grab the phone—and if it's for me, tell them I'll be done showering in, oh, less than an hour for sure."

Danny sighed slightly as she left the room, then he seemed to wake himself from his stupor, and he looked around at the surroundings. The most noticeable thing in the room was an impressively tall stack of large-denomination bank notes sitting on the desk in the corner of the room. It was more money than Danny had ever seen in his life.

Slater followed the line of his gaze and felt obliged to explain. "Old evidence," he said. "From a big counterfeit case."

Danny examined one of the bills. "Wow, it looks like the real thing."

"Sure," said Slater. "It looks real, but it turns funny colors when you burn it."

"What's it doing here?"

"I tried to use it as alimony," said Jack Slater sheepishly. "Didn't work. Hard to put one over on my ex." He opened a drawer in the desk to stash the money, then stopped. He paled slightly, staring into the drawer, as if he had seen a ghost.

Intrigued, Danny peeked to see what had thrown his friend so off balance for a moment. In a manner of speaking, Jack Slater *had* seen a ghost. In the drawer was a photograph. It was a picture of Slater and a young boy, a toddler straddling his broad shoulders. There was no doubt that this was Andrew, Slater's son who had so memorably tangled with The Ripper back in the second installment of Jack's adventures. Slater managed to wrestle his emotions back under control. He dropped the money into the drawer and slammed it. But he couldn't drive the stricken look from his eyes.

"What is it?" Danny asked.

"You wouldn't happen to have a cigar, would you?" asked Jack Slater softly.

Danny shook his head. "Sorry . . ."

Slater strode to the door. "I'll be back," he rumbled.

Danny watched him go. "You know, Jack, you don't want to overdo it."

It was a morose kind of movie magic that Jack Slater stepped into after leaving the house. Inside, it was cozy, fire burning, snug and homey. Outside, the hot, uncomfortable Santa Ana wind was blowing, raking Slater, further depressing him as he walked, head down, eyes bleak, to the corner store to buy cigars.

He didn't really want a cigar, he just wanted to get out of the house, to get away from the dispiriting moment with the photograph. But he could not drive the horrible scene from his mind . . .

The instant The Ripper had plunged the knife toward Andrew's heart, Slater's shot had slammed into the fiend's shoulder. The force of impact shoved him to the edge of the roof, and he had teetered there for a moment that lasted an eternity. For a split second, it looked like the perfect movie happy ending: The Ripper would fall to this painful death, the kid would be saved, Slater would be the big hero. As usual. But the script seemed to run off the rails in the last possible moment.

As The Ripper swayed between life and death, he managed to hook a single boney finger inside the collar of Andrew's shirt. The Ripper plummeted toward the hard ground, falling into the sea of police lights, a maelstrom flashing red, flashing blue—Andrew falling with him. Slater could still hear the scream . . .

That night on the rooftop might have been a movie to Danny, but it was all too real to Jack Slater.

ELEVEN

"He would have been about your age . . ."

Danny jumped, as if he had gotten an electric shock, quickly dropping the picture of Andrew Slater back into the desk drawer. Then he whipped around.

Whitney had not spent an hour in the shower. She was dressed now and looked knock-down, drop-dead gorgeous.

"I know," Danny said. "The Ripper killed him. Three years ago. Pulled him down. Your dad saw everything."

Whitney stared at him, perplexed, as if trying to work out something in her head. "How do you know about all that stuff?"

Danny shrugged. "Oh, you know . . . Your Dad gets in the papers a lot. I'm interested in true crime . . . So . . ."

The doorbell rang. Whitney looked a little annoyed. "That must be Skeezy."

Danny was *muy hombre*. "I'll get rid of him,"

he said like a tough guy in the . . . well, in the movies.

Trouble was, it wasn't Skeezy at the door, it was Mr. Benedict, complete with five brand-new goons, each of them armed to the teeth. Scars, tattoos and facial hair, naturally, were part of the package.

"Hello, Toto," said Mr. Benedict.

Danny threw his shoulder against the door, trying to force it closed. Unfortunately, one of the thugs pushed back and sent Danny flying back into the room. Whitney let out an ear-piercing scream, a long, shrill shriek. When her lungs emptied of air, she took a deep breath and started again.

None of the bad guys seemed too concerned about this. They fanned out into the house. One of them grabbed Danny and began frisking him roughly. Benedict threw himself into a chair and removed his sunglasses. He had yet another glass eye in his head this time, and this one seemed to have something written on it. Danny was scared, but it did occur to him that Mr. Benedict must have a whole collection of different glass eyes somewhere that he changed, from time to time, when the fancy struck him. With normal men, it was neckties or cuff links.

The thug boosted Danny's wallet from his back pocket and tossed it to Mr. Benedict, who thumbed through it as if it were a paperback book.

"Jack around?" he asked casually.

Danny thought fast. "Mr. Slater is off tracking a lead somewhere. You know."

Whitney had not stopped screaming. She was in fine voice, and if anything, she seemed to have doubled her howling power since Mr. Benedict and his ugly pals arrived.

Danny had the feeling that if she got any louder, the dogs in the neighborhood were going to start getting involved in the act. The girl was in a blind panic, and Danny couldn't quite understand it. How could a girl so cool, with a tough-looking Jeep, a hero-cop father—a movie heroine, yet—be quite so spooked. He was just a normal kid, and he was supposed to be scared, but Whitney—Whitney should be used to this.

The high pitch seemed to be annoying Mr. Benedict. He rubbed his temples, then rapped out an order. "Take her away and teach her how to shut up."

Almost involuntarily, Danny took a step forward. "Benedict!"

Mr. Benedict and his hirelings looked genuinely surprised at the note of authority in Danny's voice. In actual fact, Danny was a bit taken aback himself.

"Yes, Toto?"

Danny was pointing a warning finger. "If you so much as harm a single hair on her head . . ."

Benedict stood, crossed to Whitney, grabbed a single strand of the girl's lovely blond hair and plucked it from her head. Whitney's screaming redoubled, as if she had been burned with a red-hot poker.

Mr. Benedict returned to his armchair, held the hair between his fists and snapped it. He smiled menacingly. "You were saying?"

Danny hung his head. "Never mind."

"Get rid of her," Benedict ordered.

"Right, Boss," said one of the thugs, hustling the hysterical girl into one of the bedrooms. Danny's blood seemed to boil in his veins, but at least things were a little quieter.

Benedict waved the wallet at his captive. "I believe it was Sherlock Holmes who felt if you got rid of all logical explanations, the illogical, however impossible, was true."

"That Sherlock," said Danny.

Mr. Benedict was not in the mood for sarcasm. "I know your name is Daniel—how did you know mine?"

Danny tried to keep cool. "Slater showed me a mug shot. We made your face easy."

"Didn't anybody ever tell you it was impolite to make faces?" Benedict's voice was so cold, so calculating, that it was apparent that not even he thought the lame joke was funny. It was just something that movie villains were called upon to say every so often.

He pulled a couple of pieces of identification from Danny's wallet. One was his PS 131 ID card, the other was his New York Public Library card. The one with the big white lion on it.

"Daniel Madigan from New York City—

aren't you a long way from home? When did you get here?"

"Just," said Danny.

Benedict leaned forward in the chair, like a lawyer about to demolish a witness on the stand. "Then, pray tell, how did you know what was spoken in Vivaldi's backyard?"

Danny answered too quickly to be telling the truth, exactly. "I heard it."

"My voice travels three thousand miles? Why is it that I doubt that?"

"Um . . . I heard a recording."

Benedict sat back and stared at him. "There are microphones in the trees then?"

"You wouldn't *believe* how many."

"And the glass eye I was wearing? How did you happen to know about that?"

"I saw it," said Danny stoutly.

Mr. Benedict smiled again, as if he had heard what he wanted to hear. "The truth at last. You were, of course, hiding in those trees along with the microphones, were you not?"

Danny shook his head. "Nope. I saw it in a movie."

"A movie!"

"There are micro cameras in those trees along with the microphones."

Mr. Benedict was silent for almost a full minute. Then he said: "I have killed people younger than you. I'd try and remember that."

The thought had not, actually, ever left Danny's mind.

Benedict turned his attention back to the

contents of the wallet. Danny felt his heart beat faster as the bad guy extracted Nicky's magic ticket stub and examined it closely. He squirmed, fighting down the urge to yell: "Don't touch that!" He wanted to snatch the ticket from Benedict's hand, but he was keenly aware that the goons in the room had their guns trained on him. A movement in the wrong direction, and it was bye-bye, Danny Madigan.

Unlike everyone else here in movieland, Mr. Benedict seemed to get the vibes from the ticket. The little slip of paper fascinated him, and he turned it over and over in his hands, scrutinizing it the way a jeweler inspects a gemstone.

Danny knew he had to deflect his interest. "Look," he said from between clenched teeth. "Whatever all this is about—it's between you and Slater. There's some money in the desk . . ."

At the mention of money, all the thugs in the room became very interested.

"Take it," said Danny, "and leave me and Meredith—uh, Whitney—alone."

From the bedroom, Whitney continued her screaming monotonously.

"Is that so?" Benedict put the ticket back into the wallet and then stuffed the billfold into his own pocket. He nodded shortly toward the desk, and one of the thugs pulled open the drawer.

He grabbed the money and held it up for

Benedict to see. "Holy shit, boss. Looks like a couple of K. Easy."

Figuring that a couple of thousand dollars was nothing to Mssrs. Benedict and Vivaldi, the hood started stuffing the bills into his pockets. Benedict, in fact, did not give a damn about the money; he hardly glanced at his greedy underling. But he *did* study Danny closely. There was a gleam in the boy's eye, as if somehow he were pulling a fast one on all of them.

Suddenly, Benedict held up a hand, like a cop stopping traffic. "Wait. Give me that money."

Dang, thought the thug. He handed the money over, but very reluctantly.

Benedict studied the money as closely as he had examined the magic ticket stub. "The money is marked, isn't it?"

Danny shrugged and tried to look casual. "Marked money? No way."

There was steel in Benedict's voice. Danny didn't like the sound of it at all. "It is, isn't it, Daniel?" pressed the bad guy. "You were trying to sucker me with marked money, weren't you?"

"Me? No!" Danny did his best to look hurt, as if to say: *how could you think such a thing?*

"Don't try playing grown-up games with grown-ups, kid," said Benedict with a sneer. "You'll get hurt that way."

He grabbed the money and tossed every bill in the fire. The flames danced merrily, but all the thugs looked very sad to see that kind of cash go up in smoke.

Just then, it struck Danny that Whitney was still screaming.

But she wasn't in trouble. The first time one of the goons had hit her, she had gotten mad. It had been a hard blow, a stinging back hand smack that had bounced her into the wall and straight back into another punch. There was the slightest glimmer of blood in the fold of her lip and the beginning of a puffy purple black eye.

Whitney stopped screaming long enough to whisper two terrifying words: "Big mistake."

Still screaming, she came back at the thug with everything she had. First she speared a sharp stiletto heel square in the guy's foot, slicing through leather, flesh and bone, nailing him to the floor. The gunman stared wide-eyed, astonished at the intensity of the pain and at the ferocity of the attack. Just a second before she had been a hysterical teenage girl, now she was fighting like a tiger.

The heel of Whitney's hand seemed to zoom straight up from the floor, smashing into the point of his chin with the force of a freight train. There was an explosion of bright white deep within him, a detonation of pain in the middle of his brain. His head snapped back on his neck with a sickening crack.

Benedict's goon would never know that Whitney's screams and panic had all been part of an act, that she had been simulating the damsel-in-distress routine just long enough to get her attacker off his guard. She continued to scream as she patted down the corpse; still screaming, she boosted his gun; still screaming, she cracked open the weapon and spun the cylinder.

"That's some knife," said Danny, swallowing nervously. "Nice. Really nice."

Mr. Benedict had drawn the long, thin bone-handled silver blade from the inside pocket of his jacket and was standing over Danny, the edge just inches from his face. It hurt just *looking* at that knife. Danny tried not to look.

"Yes," Benedict agreed. "But it's not enough just to have a nice knife. You have to know how to use it too."

There was not the slightest doubt in Danny's mind that Mr. Benedict knew all about using a knife. He was probably very handy roundabout Thanksgiving.

"I'll hurt you a little bit. Just so you'll see what I mean."

"I'll take your word for it," Danny managed to stammer. He noticed that Whitney had stopped screaming. This could only be a Bad Sign.

"No. I insist." The cold steel touched his neck. Danny winced and writhed.

Then Whitney burst through the door, her gun level and true, steady and aimed straight for Benedict's head. "Freeze," she ordered.

Everything seemed to stop. The four goons in the room were taken completely off guard: not one of them was close enough to disarm her before she got off a shot, a shot that was sure to blow Benedict's head to smithereens.

"Tell them to lose the guns," said Whitney calmly, "or I redecorate in Early American Brains."

Danny felt a great burst of love in his heart. What more could a red-blooded, wholesome boy want in a woman: she was beautiful, could handle a gun, and she had a masterful command of the argot of colorful, violent threats. There wasn't a thing he would change.

But Benedict wasn't quite ready to give up. He pressed the knife to Danny's throat. "You kill me. I'll kill him," he said simply.

It was the classic Mexican standoff—and it was broken in an instant. There was a hard, insistent rapping at the front door, a noise just distracting enough to make Whitney look away for a split second.

That was all it took. One of the gunmen slapped Whitney's gun away and grabbed her by the wrists, twisting her arms behind her back. She looked to Danny and shrugged, as if to say, *I gave it my best shot . . .*

Benedict smiled. "Now then. Let's see who's at the door, shall we? And do be careful. It could be our friend Jack Slater."

Two of the hitmen moved to the door. They positioned themselves one standing on either side, then flung open the door, weapons ready.

But it wasn't Slater—as Whitney and Danny had so fervently hoped—but a nerdy-looking thin guy. He was leaning in, eyes closed and lips puckered for a kiss.

"Who the hell is *this* guy?" asked Number One Thug.

Whitney rolled her eyes. "Skeezy," she groaned.

For a second or two, everyone just stood staring at everybody else. No one had noticed that the money thrown into the fireplace a few minutes before was sending a column of bright red smoke up the chimney.

No one, that is, but Jack Slater, returning from the corner store.

The patio doors exploded inward, a tidal wave of shattered glass with a sound of a thousand volcanoes erupting simultaneously. Jack Slater had joined the party.

TWELVE

Jack Slater did not need revving up. The moment he hit the room, he was up to speed, a super-efficient machine producing high-quality mayhem.

The thugs nearest Slater were the first to get fed into the Jack Slater killing factory. He grabbed one of them in each hand, crossed his arms and squeezed his hands, pulling both triggers. The guns clutched in their fists roared, a bullet from each slamming into the other.

Slater let them drop. One flopped down into an armchair like a working stiff at the end of a long day, the other tumbled through a glass coffee table.

Bad Guy Number Three thought that he had Slater's number for sure. He had him in the cross hairs of his weapon—all he had to do was blow him away. Simple, right?

Not quite. Slater dove for the floor and rolled

113

behind the armchair as the first shots chawed great gouts of wood from the wide-plank floor. The third shot would finish him. Well, maybe not . . .

Slater acted without thinking. He ripped the cord of a floor lamp into two ragged pieces and touched the live end to the ankle of the dead thug in the armchair. The body twitched and jerked like a marionette, the dead fingers closing on the trigger of the machine pistol still clenched in its hands. A rip of five slugs tore into the body of Slater's latest attacker.

It was the twin barrels of a shotgun versus twin hard fists for the next guy. Slater got inside the weapon and smacked the bruiser back hard, the shotgun flying from his hands.

But Benedict wanted a piece of this action. Just as he raised the knife to throw it, Danny launched himself at his legs, low bridging him, bringing him down hard.

Benedict was up in a flash, but instead of rejoining the combat, he made a break for the door. Just before dashing outside, though, he did one very strange thing. Benedict smacked himself on the back of his head, popping out the glass eye. It hit the floor and bounced away, like a marble.

Danny was flabbergasted—amazed at his own bravery and astonished by Benedict's sudden burst of cowardice. Emboldened now by having taken down the toughest bad case in the room, Danny decided to help out his old pal Jack Slater.

He snatched up Benedict's knife and threw it, expecting it to fly end over end and embed itself in the chest of the last goon in the room—just like in the movies. But it didn't quite work out that way.

Bone hit bone, as the handle of the knife bonked Slater on the back of the head. It gave the tough guy just enough time to dive for his shotgun. He spun and uncorked both barrels, two streams of hot fire and lead that hit Slater squarely in the chest. The force of the blast seemed to pick him up and throw him a full five feet back across the room.

Danny felt his gorge rise and his head spin. No one, not even Jack Slater, could survive a gale-force blast from a twelve-gauge. The unthinkable had happened, and he had caused it: Jack Slater was dead for sure.

Except he wasn't.

A microsecond after hitting the ground, he was up again and firing. He had Whitney's thirty-eight, which he had found among the debris on the living-room floor. Three fast shots hit the last goon in the chest, blowing him through the picture window into the front yard of the house.

And it was over. Just like that. Silence and plaster dust hung in the air. Whitney and Danny were as still as statues, as Slater swung the gun around, covering the room, his jacket and T-shirt in tatters from the shotgun blast, showing the Kevlar body armor he wore beneath his clothes. Danny was grateful that Slater dressed for every occasion.

No one was quite sure where Skeezy was.

Then Slater caught sight of the bruise under Whitney's eye. He blinked once in astonishment, and then his features darkened. Someone had dared to hit his little girl. *Verrry* big mistake.

"I've got to catch the red eye," he intoned.

And then it started all over again. Slater headed for the door like a rocket, running for all he was worth. Danny hesitated a moment, then followed.

Or rather, tried to follow. There was no time for Jack to get to his car a few blocks away, so Slater took off on foot, pounding down the hillside, making for the freeway, a study in single-minded obsession. Arms pumping, legs churning, he ran in a straight line for the roadway, heedless of what stood between him and the men who had harmed his daughter.

Slater crossed the backyards of the neighbors, gates flying off hinges, fences smashed, his big boots chewing divots out of well-tended lawns. A watchdog opened his mouth to bark in protest—then saw Slater's face and decided otherwise.

Danny could only watch his hero disappear down the hill. Desperately he looked around him, his eyes falling on Whitney's bicycle neatly parked by the front door. It was a bright pink girl's model with gaily colored streamers decorating the grips and a white wicker basket suspended between the handlebars. The basket was decorated with a merry frieze of cavorting Smurfs. For a second, Danny wondered what a woman who could handle a weapon like a dream and drive a Jeep the size of a Hum-Vee would want with such a sweet, simple and girlish bike like the Smurfmobile over there.

Danny had a very limited experience of women so far in his short life, but he had the feeling that they would never quite make sense to him. With a sad shake of his head, he swung his leg over the pink bicycle and pedaled after his hero.

"The things I do for that guy," he said aloud.

The tough-looking Asian guy, Mr. Chew, was driving the getaway car, Benedict twisting in the passenger seat next to him. He was staring back the way they had come, half-expecting Slater to come roaring up behind them.

"Punch it," Benedict ordered. "We get to the freeway and we're home free."

"Uh . . . Boss?" said the driver.

Benedict turned and looked straight ahead over the hood of the car. Standing in the middle of the road, the Ruger Blackhawk raised and aimed, feet planted like concrete blocks, was Jack Slater. The gun bucked and fired, two hundred and forty grains of instant death smashing into the car.

The driver threw on the breaks and wrenched the wheel so violently it seemed that he would tear it from the head of the steering column. The big car lumbered into a heavy, rubber-screaming hundred-and-eighty-degree turn, fishtailing on the asphalt. Slater had not moved, the gun blasting big slugs into the body work of the car, tearing out hot chunks of metal. It was the closest you could get to being attacked by anti-aircraft fire and still be on the ground.

Mr. Chew managed to keep the car on course. He stamped on the gas, and the car vaulted forward, back up the hill, the way it had come a second or two before.

Danny was coming down the hill when he heard the gunshots and the squeal of rubber.

"Jack! Where are you?" He shook his head, frustrated. "I don't believe it! I'm in an action movie and I'm missing the best action!"

Danny was not, at that stage of his life, acquainted with the expression "Be careful what you wish for . . . You may get it." It was just as well that he didn't know the saying.

As he turned the corner, he saw Benedict's car rushing up the hill, straight at him, as if the big sedan were locked on the puny bicycle like a Smurf-seeking missile. Half a mile and closing.

"Omigod!" yelped Danny. Then his hands clenched on the handlebar grips, the streamers fluttering out beside him. He swallowed hard. "Chicken. Chicken it is!"

He started to pedal, slowly at first, then with more determination, picking up speed on the downgrade. His mouth was set in a grim fighter-ace-facing-certain-death line. He was totally un-aware of how ridiculous he looked, as a two-ton automobile bore down on a pink girl's five-speed. Decorated with Smurfs.

Collision was imminent. Danny was sweating. He closed his eyes and chanted his mantra: "This is going to work. This is going to work. This is a movie. I'm a good guy. This has got to work."

He opened his eyes, and the cold, god-awful, undeniable truth hit him a few seconds before the car would. "I'm the comedy sidekick! Oh shit, I'm the comedy sidekick. *It's not gonna work!*"

Danny swerved and jumped the road, feeling the hot wind of the car—and certain death—blast over him. The bike tumbled down the hillside, sliding down the steep slope until it landed in a heap on the roadway below. Danny was sprawled next to the wreckage of Whitney's bicycle, his eyes closed tight—he was afraid that if he opened them, he would find himself dead anyway.

Then he smelled cigar smoke. Dead guys couldn't smell anything, as far as he knew. He opened an eye. Slater was standing over him.

"I think I scared 'em pretty good," said Danny.

Slater shook his head, then reached down and hauled Danny up, slinging him over his shoulder like a duffel bag. He started marching up the hill, the mangled bike in his other hand.

Danny was limp on Slater's broad shoulder,

thankful to be alive after the hair-raising events of the last twelve minutes—it was amazing how much action you could pack into so little time, he thought. Of course, being in a movie helped. In real life you wouldn't be able to take quite so many shortcuts . . . Then it hit him. *Real life*. The worst thing that could happen in all this *had* happened. Benedict had stolen his wallet—it seemed an eternity ago— and that meant . . .

"Benedict has the ticket," said Danny, his voice sick. Now what was he going to do? He wondered what time it was back in the real world. His mother would kill him . . . His mother would be worried to death.

"Too bad," growled Slater, still unconvinced by all this movie stuff. "That's a shame, I really wanted it for my collection."

But Danny was too worn out to argue with the man. Besides, it felt pretty good to be carried to safety.

Although things weren't exactly cozy when they got back to the house. The entire street and the front lawn were packed with police cars and emergency rescue vehicles. A helicopter circled above, the spotlight cutting through the dusk to sweep the crime scene.

Inside, things were worse. Extended shootouts make such a mess. There was shattered glass and splintered furniture everywhere, not to mention shattered and splintered tough guys. The bodies were being loaded onto stretchers and carried out to the wagons of the county coroner. Uniformed cops were sweeping the room for evidence.

Slater looked over the wreckage and then sat down next to the sole unbroken window and sullenly smoked his cigar. Bruised and battered and definitely in a bad mood, Jack didn't look as if he wanted any part of the busy doings going on around him.

Danny had revived a bit, and with the return of his energy came the desire to prove to Jack Slater he was in a movie. Besides, he wanted to take a crack at cheering up his friend. And there was no better way Danny knew to cheer Jack up than to demonstrate that he was not a screwed-up cop whose antics had gotten his daughter beaten up by thugs, but a big screen hero beloved by millions.

Danny had an idea. He grabbed a piece of paper and a pen from the desk and quickly wrote a word—an extremely obscene and bad word beginning with the letter *F*—on it.

This he thrust under Slater's nose. "Say this," he ordered.

Slater glanced at the paper and looked disgusted. "Grow up, why don't you?"

Danny did his best to coax him. "Just say this one word. For me."

Slater shook his head, offended. "Is this another of your movie proofs?"

"Maybe," said Danny coyly.

"Kid, I don't want to say it."

"Say what?"

Slater shot him a look easily as dirty as the

word scrawled on the piece of paper. "Get lost, kid."

Danny was triumphant. "You can't, can you? You can't possibly say it because this movie is PG-13. Go on, admit it."

Slater turned his back on him huffily. "I don't have to admit anything."

"Like hell."

"Watch your mouth."

"Detective Slater?" It was Skeezy. When the shooting started, he had dived for cover and had stayed there until well after it stopped.

"Yeah?"

"The guy with the missing eye?" said Skeezy, hoping he was being helpful. "I saw part of his license plate number."

Big deal, thought Slater. "Good for you . . . Wait . . . You mean the guy with the *glass* eye?"

Skeezy was puzzled. "No. He had one eye the last time I saw him."

"Oh yeah," Danny chimed in. "That's right. I forgot to mention—"

On the far side of the room a uniformed police officer was reaching down for the small, dark orb. "I got it." He picked it up and held it close. "There's something written on it. It says: 'Vengeance is mine.' What's that?"

"Don't touch that!" yelled Slater. Then he added: *"Bomb!"*

The glass eye detonated, and the entire room was suddenly awash in smoke and flame. The blast was deafening. There were screams and yells as bodies went flying.

By Danny's reckoning, it was his second major explosion of the day.

Benedict was not feeling so good. He made it back to his quarters at Tony Vivaldi's mansion and locked himself in. The ace assassin was feeling even more spooked than before. He didn't care for the sensation—it was not a common state of mind for people in his line of work. Something about that kid bothered him mightily, and he couldn't figure out what it was.

Without thinking about it—he was hardly aware he had done it—Benedict snapped on the big television set in the corner of his room, then dropped into a chair. Maybe the wallet held a clue. He pulled it out and started going through the contents carefully.

There was nothing there you wouldn't expect to find in a kid's wallet. Minimal cash. The school ID and the library card he had seen already. The bus pass was normal; so was the photograph of the dark-haired middle-aged woman Benedict took to be Danny's mother.

That left the ticket. There was something about this glowing scrap of paper that fascinated him. Still holding it, Benedict stood up and paced the room back and forth, all the while staring at the object in his hand.

He just couldn't figure it out, and he shook his head, confused. Benedict stopped and leaned against the wall, pausing to think . . . But instead of resting on the wall, his hand passed right through!

Panicked, Benedict pulled his hand back and looked at it. It was fine. Nothing had changed . . . except he had the power to pass through solid matter. The ticket glowed in his other hand, almost winking at him, daring him to figure out what was going on.

The TV provided the answer. A program was just coming on. Rod Serling's unmistakable voice: "You're traveling to another dimension, a dimension of mind . . ."

Then the theme from "The Twilight Zone" started: *Doo-doo/doo-doo/doo-doo/doo-doo* . . . Benedict smiled. It was the perfect end to an otherwise lousy day.

THIRTEEN

Lieutenant Dekker was so angry that he kept on changing color. It was a process that Danny watched with great interest, seeing as he couldn't really make much sense of what Dekker was saying.

He and Slater were standing in the lieutenant's office, both of them with a little of that black smudge on their foreheads and chins that is movie sign language for "I have undergone a huge explosion but luckily escaped with nothing more serious than minor cuts and bruises."

"Goddammit, Slater!" Dekker roared. "I've got the Governor's office baby-sitting my furry walnuts. I've got the California Raisin Council doing the all-male production of "The Diary of Anne Frank in my fuzzy pumper. Tiny Tim is tiptoeing through my tulips!"

Danny noted that Dekker had changed from his normal brown to black and was now well on his way to a kind of blue-green. Fascinating.

"Do I make myself clear?" Dekker bellowed.

Slater whispered to Danny, "Does this make any sense to you?"

"Uh . . . No," said Danny, shaking his head.

But Dekker was far from finished. In fact, he seemed angrier, as if his own words had driven him to an even greater frenzy. He seemed to throw off heat like a radiator.

"You ball-peen jackamenace!" he screamed. "I've slurped about all the cock toasting I can take from you poncey poon fackers! You take the shingles off the monkey stick!"

"I'm almost sure it's English," murmured Danny. He added: "Well, it's only a *guess*."

Every single one of Dekker's muscles seemed to swell, and suddenly he appeared to be one-and-a-half times life size. "See if this is plain enough for you: Slater, *gimme your badge!*"

Jack Slater was stunned, although Danny couldn't quite understand why. Slater lost his badge in every movie, only to win it back with amazing heroics in the last reel. How could he not know that?

"But Lieutenant, I—"

"No buts, Slater! Hand it over! I swear, this time you'll never get it back. Never! Not as long as I'm on this police force! I can't make it any plainer than that. Now, gimme the badge."

Slater slid the leather wallet containing his beloved badge across the desk. Dekker seized it, threw it into a desk drawer and slammed it shut.

"Now, get the hell out of here and clean out your desk!"

Slater turned and stormed out of Dekker's office, stomping back into the squad room and throwing himself behind his desk. For a moment, all activity in the room stopped, Slater's fellow detectives staring at him for a second or two to see if Jack would attempt to shoot anyone. When it became apparent that he would not, the bustle started up again.

The watch commander was once again at his task of assigning mismatched pairs of cops. It seemed that this was the main part of his job.

"Wohlschleager!" the grizzled old cop yelled. "You're partnered up with the black-and-white digitalization of Humphrey Bogart as Sam Spade."

Danny gaped as the black-and-white figure of Humphrey Bogart in the classic trench coat and snap-brim fedora swaggered up to his new partner.

"Hey, Joe," the old movie star rasped. "Whaddya know?"

"Wow," Danny gasped. "It's just like a commercial for Diet Coke."

Slater wasn't interested. This was just business as usual, as far as he was concerned. He concentrated on sweeping his few personal belongings into a duffel bag.

The watch commander was consulting his assignment clipboard again. Danny couldn't wait to see what happened next.

"Mitchell! You'll be working with Watson." The two detectives eyed each other awkwardly. It was obvious that there was something wrong with this paring. There was no odd-couple element at all—both men were about the same age, about the same build. Both men were black.

Mitchell turned to the watch commander. "Uh, Sarge . . . ?" he said a little flustered. "I hate to bring this up but . . . We're both . . . uh . . ."

The watch commander slapped his forehead. "Oh. Sorry. Wasn't thinking."

John Practice, Slater's old FBI pal, wandered over to Slater and perched on the edge of the desk.

"I'm working the funeral," he said. "How about you, Jack?"

Slater shook his head.

"I wouldn't miss this one. I've seen some mob funerals in my time, but this one should top them all. I heard Torelli spent a damn bundle. He'd got a damn helicopter circling the building. A rooftop service. How's that for taste?"

Slater couldn't resist asking. "Who died?"

"Leo the Fart."

Slater's eyebrows shot up. "Leo? I don't believe it."

Practice nodded. "Believe it. He got shot yesterday. Someone was trying for Torelli and missed."

Slater was very impressed. "Leo was tough."

"I'll say." Practice started for the door. "You change your mind about being at the funeral, Jack, I'll be at the gate."

Slater seemed genuinely moved at the news of Leo the Fart's sudden demise. He cleared the last of his possessions into the bag.

"You knew this guy Leo?" asked Danny.

"Yep. Leo could do anything but sneak up on you. Let's get out of here."

Slater drove sedately and in silence across the city, stopping for all the red lights and keeping within the speed limits. No crashes, no gunfire, not even an explosion. It was as if all that action just vanished the minute you stopped being a cop. Finally, Slater pulled the car to a halt in front of an ugly, featureless concrete apartment building situated in a marginal neighborhood.

Danny looked around. "Where are we?"

"Home," said Slater.

"Home" looked just as bad inside as it did from the outside. Slater's apartment was almost completely empty. No pictures decorated the gray walls. No books, no stereo, no TV. The only furniture was a single mattress on the floor. A telephone sat next to it.

There was a closet. The instant Jack and Danny entered the apartment, Slater unholstered his Ruger Blackhawk and fired two quick shots into the closet. The noise was deafening, and Danny nearly jumped out of his skin.

But before the roar had died away, a gunman tumbled out of the closet. Dead. Apparently he hadn't heard the news about Slater being off the force.

"Jeez!" yelped Danny. "How did you know there was a guy in there?"

Jack Slater sighed wearily. "There's always a guy in there." He shook his head. "Costs me a fortune in closet doors."

"That's right! Like in *Slater II*, the Sagittarius Strangler. You remember the part where—"

But Slater wouldn't listen. He tossed the duffel bag into the closet until recently occupied by the late hitman. "Kid," he said. "The show is over. What you find so entertaining . . . It's my life. And I'm not even a cop now." He shut the closet door, then leaned against the wall, slowly sliding down it till he was resting on the floor.

Danny sat down next to him, sad to see his hero so low. "I promise you, you'll get your badge back—Dekker was just pulling rank because you've been destroying more of the city than usual, that's all."

"I've never seen him so mad before. Did you notice he was changing color? It was all I could do to be casually irreverent."

"Jack," implored Danny, "I swear—you're not just *my* hero, you're *everybody's* hero. You'll see. Everything is going to be great again. I promise."

Slater shook his head slowly. He looked tired and deeply melancholy. "It's getting harder, Danny. I never started out to be anything but a decent cop. Then I kept getting involved in these crazy adventures—but the craziest things was, I kept on surviving them."

Danny listened, tears in his eyes. Could it be that the great Jack Slater was just giving up? It was plainly the end of civilization as he knew it.

"Last month," Slater continued quietly. "These two virgin nuns were trapped in a burning building and Dekker said 'Slater, climb up the outside and rescue them.' So I did."

"But-but . . . *that's great.*" Danny couldn't quite place the incident, though, in his Jack Slater filmography.

Slater shrugged. "I guess . . . but I never climbed the outside of a building before. I almost fell off a half a dozen times. I was exhausted when I got home. Took six Advil to stop my head from throbbing."

"But you weren't . . ." Danny could scarcely bring himself to say the word. "You weren't *scared* were you?"

Slater looked at him as if he did not know the meaning of the word *fear*. "No, of course not."

"Whew . . ." said Danny.

"I wasn't scared. But so what?"

"Try to look on the bright side," said Danny, trying to sound chirpy. "Count your blessings.

You've got a great daughter, and your ex-wife wouldn't keep calling if somewhere deep down she didn't want you back."

The look on Slater's face told Danny that he had probably said the wrong thing. Jack, it seemed, did not like to be reminded about his family.

"Do you think I'd be married to someone so stupid they couldn't tell a real voice from a tape that keeps going 'uh-huh'?"

"Guess not," said Danny. But he was still puzzled. "Then who is it that calls you?"

"I pay the cashier at the drugstore to call me."

"Not your ex-wife?"

Slater shook his head. "No. My ex-wife is very happily remarried to an orthodontist. She didn't want any alimony. Nothing. She *never* calls."

"Well, what about Whitney? She's certainly—"

Slater cut him off. He was getting angry now, his voice louder. "And Whitney! If she could just be like other teenagers—but noooo. She only enjoys pistol practice and karate class."

Jack Slater the super-cop had disappeared and had been replaced with Jack Slater the disappointed parent. Danny found this slightly unnerving. As for Whitney's faults—these were all part of her charm.

"She can beat up every boy she dates," Slater continued. "And they all know it. So they don't call, 'cause they're afraid she'll hurt them. Look at how she was looking forward to the arrival of that nerd Skeezy!"

There's always me, thought Danny.

Jack Slater gave a huge, sad sigh. "Whitney is going to die a young maid, I just know it." It seemed that Jack Slater was feeling the tiniest bit sorry for himself. "I'm going to buy it soon too."

Danny shook his head vigorously. "Don't you understand? You can't die till the grosses start falling off." Danny was striving mightily to cheer up his idol. "Listen, we all get blue—I get mugged and I get depressed. You, you haven't blown anything up for hours. You feel like a failure, but it'll pass . . ."

Danny's voice trailed off. He could see that his pep talk was not having the desired effect at all. Then he had a brilliant idea. The way to cheer Jack Slater up was not with some *I'm-okay-You're-okay* psychobabble. The thing that would work with him was more *I'm a psychotic-You-have-a-big-gun.*

"That guy Vivaldi," said Danny slyly. "I heard him say something was going to happen at a funeral. And now this Leo the Fart is going to have one. Pretty strange coincidence, don't you think?"

In spite of his glum mood, Slater did find his interest piqued. "But he didn't say what, did he?"

"Well, no. I couldn't watch long enough to tell. But he did say that when Tony Vivaldi plans a bloodbath, there's a bloodbath. That should count for something, right?"

"A bloodbath." Nothing perked Jack Slater up like the promise of a good massacre. He began to show a hint of energy. "What if you're right?"

He grabbed the phone and punched in a number quickly. Movie logic was beginning to kick in—that quality that certain movie characters had to have, that isolated, brilliant, but heretofore unimagined, insight that set the plot rolling again.

"What if they fed my second cousin Frank the wrong information on purpose, knowing it would get back to me?"

"Yeah!" said Danny.

"This is Slater," he barked into the phone. "Read me the list of break-ins in the last twenty-four hours." He listened. "No, no, no, no—*yes!* That's it." He slammed down the phone.

"What's going on?" asked Danny.

"There was a break-in at Tofutti's mortuary last night." Slater was racing for the door.

"So?" said Danny, trying to keep up.

"So Leo the Fart was laid out at the mortuary."

It was the old Slater. He jumped behind the wheel of the Bonneville and they roared away, dashing across the city, the speed never dropping below sixty.

"Jack, what's happening?"

Slater had it all figured out. Movie logic never let him down. "Check this out: someone tried to kill Old Man Torelli, right? Missed and shot Leo the Fart by mistake."

Danny was enjoying the ride, holding on tight. "That's right."

"Uh-uh. Wrong," shouted Slater. "Who took the shot? Was it Benedict? Probably. Would he miss? You know Benedict. He wouldn't miss. No way. *Not unless he wanted to miss*."

"You're saying he meant to kill Leo? Why?" He was one of nature's noble sidekicks, that Danny Madigan.

"Because, amigo . . . Leo the Fart was very, very fat. Get it?"

Danny shook his head. "No, I don't." The kid was a natural, to sidekickness born.

"They broke in last night. Cut Leo open like a turkey and stuffed him with TNT. He goes off to the funeral, he takes out the entire Torelli mob. *All at once*. And if that happens, Vivaldi owns the town."

Danny's eyes glowed. "Oh. Oh, wow!" His mind was racing, digesting the information he had just heard. There was just one thing wrong with the data.

"No . . . no . . ." Danny said, thinking hard. "It wouldn't be just a bomb. We've already had a dozen explosions in this movie."

Jack Slater glowered. "No, don't start, Danny—" Then it hit him. "Nerve gas."

"What?"

"Three canisters of nerve gas were stolen

from military trucks the night before last. They could have stuffed those inside him!" Slater shot a glance at Danny. "And you know what that means, don't you?"

"No."

"Leo the Fart is going to pass gas one more time."

FOURTEEN

Mob funerals followed their own fashion dictates, but one rule was always supreme: the gaudier, the more eye-grabbing, the better. The idea was that if you got killed in the line of duty, then all of your pals and, often, the people who killed you, would show up to see you off. Leo, having been right-hand man to Mr. Torelli himself—and having been rubbed out taking a slug for the boss—was going to get the grand send-off his life and death so richly merited.

Torelli had pulled out all the stops, sparing no expense for the funeral of his beloved lieutenant. The funeral was set up on the roof of a large hotel, twelve stories above the street, overlooking the sprawl of Los Angeles. The most notable feature of the hotel was the set of glass-enclosed elevators that ran up and down the exterior of the building. The hotel was not situated in that great a neighborhood. There was a lot of construction going on, and the building sat next to one of the bubbling black tar pits that dotted the greater LA area.

Although it was supposed to be a funeral, the whole setting looked more like some kind of elaborate party. There were flowers everywhere, and the entire roof was ringed with flags and streamers that snapped and waved in the stiff breeze. In the sky above the rooftop, a helicopter clattered, endlessly circling the scene below.

Hundreds of friends, family members and former associates of the deceased had gathered on the rooftop, standing in little clusters talking among themselves. From time to time, men in shiny dark suits would walk up to Don Torelli to pay their respects.

Of course, the center of attention was the late Leo the Fart. He was resplendent in a giant bronze coffin the size of a packing crate, along the lines of something that had once contained a commercial deep freeze. Considering the shape he was in, Leo looked pretty good. The undertaker had made up his face, and he had even massaged a little smile into his fat lips.

Happy at his own funeral—that was Leo all over. Of course, he wasn't the only one who looked happy attending the ceremony. Old Man Torelli was standing in the middle of his knot of bodyguards and cronies, accepting the respects of the mourners, and he smiled warmly when Tony Vivaldi and Mr. Benedict approached.

"Mr. Torelli," said Tony Vivaldi with a little bow, "I hope it's all right with you I'm here. I wouldn't want to be a fourth wheel." Vivaldi knew that he had to do this phoney respect thing. Old dons like Torelli went for that kind of old-fashioned thing.

Benedict, hanging back a few feet, rolled his eyes behind his very dark glasses and muttered, "That's *fifth* wheel, you moron."

Old Man Torelli waved away Vivaldi's niceties. "Nonsense, Antonio. You honor me with your presence here. Now that we're partners, we're family."

Vivaldi smiled broadly, and he smacked Benedict hard on the shoulder. "You hear that, Mr. Benedict? Family. Now, go and pay your respects."

Benedict forced a smile onto his face and nodded to his boss. He strode over to Leo and leaned over the coffin, reverently kissing the dead hand of the corpse. He had a quick look around to make sure that no one was paying attention and then yanked once on Leo's little finger. There was a perceptible "click" followed by a faint beep. The bomb buried deep in Leo's capacious gut had been activated.

The Pontiac Bonneville screeched to a halt at the curb right next to the funeral site. Slater threw open the door.

"Stay in the car," he ordered Danny.

"Stay in the car? No way. I'm coming with you."

Slater leaned on the top of the door. "Kid, if this is a movie—"

"It *is*," insisted Danny. "Really."

"Okay, say it is a movie, just for the sake of argument. How many times have you heard someone in a movie say 'Stay in the car,' but the guy doesn't? What happens?"

"Easy," said Danny. "He shows up at the last minute and saves the day."

"True," said Slater. "Or he gets killed, and then the hero has to vow to avenge him. It's the thing that drives him all the way through the rest of the movie."

Danny had to agree. "Good point. I'll stay in the car."

"I knew you would see it my way."

"Wait! What if staying in the car is the very thing that gets me killed?"

Slater called over his shoulder: "There's a gun in the glove compartment."

No kidding. Danny opened the glove compartment and a torrent of weapons poured out, a clattering flow of lethal steel. There were a couple of guns, along with brass knuckles, knives, Ninja throwing stars, num-chuks and a hand grenade. Danny grabbed a gun and felt much better.

Practice was hanging around the main entrance to the hotel, as if waiting for someone. Turned out he was waiting for Slater.

"Hey, Practice!"

"Makes perfect," said the FBI man. "So you decided to join me after all, huh?"

Slater nodded. "Had to. The Fart is a bomb. He's gonna take out the whole Torelli mob. We gotta stop it."

Suddenly it all made sense to Practice. "That explains the break in at the mortuary. Jesus, that's brilliant." The fed was all action. "Come on! We'll use the service elevator in the back of the building."

Slater didn't hesitate. He followed Practice around the corner and into the alley next to the hotel. As soon as they got there, Jack stopped.

"Who the hell are you working for, John?"

"What does that mean?"

"I mean, there's no side entrance to this building. I know it. You know it."

Practice's answer was to pull a gun. "I'm sorry, Jack. I didn't want it to go down this way."

Slater's face had turned to stone. "Danny said not to trust you. Said you had killed Moe Zart."

Practice's forehead wrinkled, trying to place the name. "I kill a lot of people—I can't remember half of them." He cocked the gun. "I want you to know this, Slater—this isn't personal, Jack. Strictly business."

Suddenly a voice rang out. "How do you get to Carnegie Hall?"

Practice glanced over his shoulder. Danny was standing at the head of the alley, his gun pointed straight at Practice. The FBI man smiled.

"Suppose you tell me, kid."

"In a body bag, if you don't drop that piece," said Danny, hoping his voice sounded like that of a twelve-year-old cold-blooded killer, with plenty of corpses to his credit. This was where he was going to find out which role he was going to play: savior or the guy who gets killed in a suitably inspirational manner. Danny was really betting on savior.

"Doubtful." Practice kept his weapon trained on Slater, but he moved fast on Danny. To Danny's dismay, he noticed that his hand had start to vibrate, telegraphing the fear he was feeling deep in his bones.

Practice tore the weapon from Danny's hand, grasping it by the barrel. "Congratulations, kid." Practice really seemed to be enjoying himself. "You just killed Jack Slater."

"I did? No way."

"Your prints are on this gun, aren't they?"

"Oh. Yeah. I guess."

John Practice pulled a pair of handcuffs from the pocket of his gray FBI-type suit coat. He tossed them to Danny. "Here. Chain yourself to the pipe."

"Second time today . . . tonight," muttered Danny. He clicked the cuffs shut around his thin wrist. "Damn." This was too much like real life.

Practice had tucked his own gun into the small of his back and had the drop on Slater with Danny's weapon, holding it in a handker-chief to keep the fingerprints pristine. Made things nice and neat for the evidence cops.

"See, Jack, these drug guys . . . they've got a lot of more money than the U.S. Government."

"So you cut a deal with a Sicilian scumbag like Tony Vivaldi? Is that it?"

Danny looked on helplessly. Things had been going so well up till now. The thought of seeing Jack Slater gunned down by an officer of the law, by the man he had saved in Vietnam, it was just sickening.

Then he remembered something. If this had been a cartoon, a little light bulb would have gone on over his head. He still had the handcuff key, the one from the real world. The one the punk had tossed in the toilet. And to think that he had been disappointed when the real-world cop didn't want it as a piece of evidence!

"I guess I owe you an explanation," said Practice. "I'll explain it all to you. It doesn't matter, since you're going to die anyway."

"Suppose you do that," growled Slater.

"You see, Vivaldi made up with Torelli, but it was false—he's going to destroy him—so in exchange for letting him alone, he gives me a profit percentage. I'll be rich, Jack. I'll be rich and you'll be dead."

Danny had fished the key out of his pocket and unlocked the cuffs. He creeped along the alley and grabbed Practice's gun from the waistband of his pants.

"Freeze!"

That was all the daylight Slater needed. He slapped Practice's gun from his hand, twisted his arm behind his back and slammed him into the hard brick wall.

"Danny, toss me the cuffs."

While Slater locked up the rogue FBI man, Danny held the gun on him.

"God, Practice, you are such an idiot!" Danny squealed. "You made the classic movie mistake. *Don't explain so much*. You had us. You could have just killed us, but no, you had to tell us everything. Just had to get in those last words." Danny rolled his eyes.

"Look at this," mumbled Practice. "I'm getting busted by Pauline Kael."

Danny continued his harangue. "If you'd just fired, you'd have won, but no, you're just the typical villain—dumb."

"You ain't no genius yourself, kid." It was Vivaldi and Benedict. Both had guns out—and they would use them if they had to. "You just made the same mistake."

It took only seconds for a quick exchange of guns—although it was rather one-sided. The good guys gave theirs to the bad guys, who kept them.

Benedict checked his watch. "The Fart goes off in seven minutes."

"Go get the car," Vivaldi ordered. "Now. Move it. Chop-chop."

Benedict did not enjoy being spoken to in this manner, particularly by a man he considered his inferior. Still, Benedict was anxious to get out of the neighborhood before the climate changed. He did what he was told.

Vivaldi cackled gleefully. "Well, I'd love to stay and watch the fun, but I have to go and establish my alibi. *Arrivederci,* you guys." He turned and sidled down the alley, around the corner and out of sight.

It was just Slater, Danny and Practice now.

"Is this the day you talked about saving?" Slater stage-whispered to Danny.

"I don't see *you* doing anything."

"Wouldn't want to steal your thunder," said Slater.

FIFTEEN

Practice was completely in control now. His gun was leveled at the back of Slater's head, ready to blow him away.

"Gentlemen," he said, "someone once told me that I talk too much." He cocked the weapon. "Now, no more words."

There were two blasts, and Danny was sure he was dead—but he wasn't. As one, he and Slater turned and saw Practice dropping to his knees, two fatal shots staining his FBI-issue white shirt. At the far end of the alley stood the Animated Cat, a smoking revolver clutched in his paw.

Slater checked his watch. "Whiskers! Where the hell have you been?"

"Sorry, Jack. Got held up. Animated mouse."

The cat tossed Slater a gun. "Thanks, Whiskers. I owe you one."

"Forget it," said Whiskers gruffly. "You've saved my fur plenty of times."

Slater was on his knees frisking Practice. Quickly, he pocketed the erstwhile G-man's gun, badge and a couple of cheap cigars. "Whiskers! Seal off the area. We got a possible chemical explosion in five minutes."

"What do *I* do?" said Danny, a little bewildered.

Slater pointed to the huge crane parked on the construction site across the street from the hotel. A heavy hook at the end of a long chain dangled from the hoist. "That. That hook needs to be at the roof in two minutes. Go."

Danny looked at the crane and blanched. "How do I get them to do that?"

Slater had answers for anything, many of them having to do with guns. He handed Practice's weapon to Danny. "Maybe you can persuade them."

"Right!" Danny grabbed the firearm and started running, charging toward the construction site. He was sure that even with a gun, he would be hard-pressed to convince the construction workers that he needed their crane—now!—and that he meant business.

As it happened, it was a lot easier than he had thought it was going to be. The burly guy operating the controls of the crane nearly jumped out of his skin when he saw a very small boy carrying a very large weapon bearing down on him, screaming at the top of his voice.

"Move that crane over to the roof of the hotel!" Danny shouted, waving the pistol.

It was in the papers every day—ninety thousand kids in LA had handguns, and a lot of them used them—and the construction guy believed what he read in the papers. Why hang around? Unceremoniously, he abandoned his post, taking to his heels and running for safety.

Danny had done his job too well. It had been his plan—insofar as he *had* a plan—to get the crane operator to . . . operate the crane.

"Wait!" he shouted. "Stop! How do I work this thing?" Danny scanned the absurdly complicated controls. "I don't even know how to drive."

In the center of the instrument panel was a lever, like a joystick from an airplane cockpit. It looked like a promising place to start. Danny put down his gun and started wrestling with the control, and to his amazement, the machine shuddered and groaned, the long arm beginning to rotate and move.

Slater rode the glass elevator to the roof and stepped into the middle of the funeral looking totally out of place. Cops never felt welcome at mob funerals, and even less so if they were improperly dressed, in tattered jeans and cowboy boots. Some of the mourners looked askance and muttered darkly in a language Slater didn't understand.

But he was a man with a mission. He plunged into the crowd, elbowing his way through the pack of mourners lined up to pay their respects to the late Leo the Fart.

"'Scuse me, pardon me . . . ," Slater muttered, shoving his way through the crowd. "Pardon me, 'scuse me . . . Sorry. 'Scuse me."

It didn't take him long to shoulder his way to the casket, where he stood for a moment looking somber and reverent.

"Leo . . . ," he said with a heavy sigh. "He was a good man . . . He was a flatulent man . . ."

Suddenly, Slater frowned, a look of great puzzlement crossing his face. "Wait! Did you hear that?" He asked the people around him. Maybe it was the helicopter making a pass over the scene, but no one seemed to have heard anything.

"Hear what?" some gangster demanded.

Slater leaned down and put his ear close to Leo's mouth, as if listening to the man whisper to him. Then he stared dumbstruck at the bloated face of the corpse.

"Help! Get me outta here! Hey, someone get me out of this thing!" It was Jack Slater's first foray into the field of ventriloquism—and not a very professional one—but the effects were immediate.

Slater stood bolt upright and turned to the crowd. "My God! This man is *not* dead!"

Under the cover of the furor he had created among the mourners, Slater started prying the giant dead mobster from the casket. He wrestled the three-hundred-pound bulk onto his shoulders and started to run for the edge of the building.

"Quick! Out of my way! This man needs a doctor!"

The crowd parted, allowing Slater a good shot at getting out of there without being hindered. There were a number of reasons that people were getting out of the way. Some were just bewildered and got out of the way because someone was yelling at them to do that. Other mourners genuinely believed that Leo had come back to life and was in dire need of medical attention. The vast majority of the throng, though, thought it prudent to give a wide berth to a nut who broke into a funeral and stole the guest of honor.

Dead ahead of him the skyhook was jerkily cutting through the sky toward the hotel roof. Slater headed for it at a dead run, legs pumping.

"I need a doctor!" he yelled.

An elderly man stepped directly into his path. "I am a doctor," he said.

Jack Slater had not counted on a doctor being in attendance at a mob funeral. But, as said, Slater had answers for just about everything—and if the answer wasn't a gun, it was frequently a fist.

"Look at his chin," Jack ordered.

"His chin?" The doctor bent to look, leaning straight into Slater's lightning jab. The doctor went out like a light.

"The doctor has fainted! Somebody help this man! I'll take the corpse—uh, patient—" He looked around quickly and could tell that he was beginning to lose his crowd. Guns were appearing here and there, and that could only be a bad sign.

"Look!" Slater yelled. *"An elephant!"* It was all he could think of. He jumped straight for the ledge of the roof, teetering there, reaching for the hook.

Behind him a hundred guns had been unholstered and were pointed at Slater's back.

"Easy!" someone shouted. "Don't shoot. He'll drop Leo."

Danny hadn't quite mastered the controls of the construction crane. The hook was coming in fast, but unfortunately, he couldn't stop it in time. The big grapple swung right by Jack and on into the crowd of gangsters, knocking some of them flying like nine pins. Desperate, Danny slammed the lever in reverse, and the hook changed direction, swung back the way it had come and dropped below the level of the roofline.

Slater swore horribly, rapidly changing the MPAA rating of this particular movie. All one hundred guns on the roof cocked and were ready to blow Slater over the edge.

Jack froze on the brink of the roof and turned slowly, raising his arms as he did so. "Wait," he implored. "Don't shoot."

The crowd didn't shoot. They gasped. In raising his arms, Slater had tipped Leo's lifeless body, dropping him over the edge of the building. As one, the crowd broke for the rail to see what happened when Leo hit the ground.

But he hadn't made it that far. Leo was on the hook, his collar snagged, his head lolling and, they could see, as dead as a doornail. Leo was on the hook, and Jack Slater was running for the elevator.

There was no time for Jack to deal with such elevator niceties as using the door. He vaulted over the lip of the roof and dropped a story or two to the top of the elevator. He hit the top of the capsule, the glass spider-webbing under the impact. The force of the jolt as he struck almost shook him off the rapidly descending car, but he managed to hang on with one hand, yanking himself back up on top.

The roar of the helicopter filled Slater's ears. It was coming around now, and he could see it, stubby little machine guns projecting from the skids. It was definitely time to get out of there.

The Ruger Blackhawk appeared in his hands like magic, and he fired a single big slug into the lock of the elevator escape hatch. Slater dropped into the elevator cab and hit every button on the control panel.

"Ding." The elevator stopped and the doors opened. Slater lurched forward and stopped. The entire hotel seemed to be filled with gangsters; more were tumbling down the stairs.

"Oooops," said Slater. He threw himself flat just as the chopper's machine guns opened up. The guns chattered, pumping a hundred rounds into the lobby, firing over Slater, but slicing through the ranks of mobsters.

"Ding." The elevator doors closed again, and

the cab dropped. But the chopper rotated, nose down, following the elevator as it plummeted toward the ground floor. Slater was trapped, the helicopter just outside the capsule, huge and menacing. The guns were locked on him. They couldn't miss . . .

Until—out of nowhere—came the skyhook, Leo still dangling on the end like obese bait on a giant fishing line. The chain clipped the rear rotor of the helicopter, and there was an immediate scream of tortured metal and motor. Guns blazing, smoke pouring from the machine, the helicopter careened out of control.

Bullets spattered the side of the building, sawing a hot line of lead in the face of the hotel, just above the elevator. But not a single slug touched Slater.

The chopper was spinning crazily toward the ground. It hit the street and detonated in a cloud of black smoke and flame.

"Bye-bye," said Slater.

But his troubles were far from over. The helicopter had done enough damage to the elevator housing to wreck it almost completely. Suddenly the top of the elevator pulled free, spilling Jack Slater out into thin air.

The fall seemed to take half an hour, but in fact, lasted less than a second. This time, in free-fall, Slater figured for sure that his number had finally been called.

But it hadn't. There was one last trick. Slater's fist closed around Leo the Fart's ankle. He swung wildly for a minute and, because of the gangster penchant for wearing silk socks, had only an uncertain, rather slippery grip.

Slater managed to hang on long enough to shout to Danny: "Stop the crane when I tell you!"

Danny, feeling a little more confident and assured at the controls, now that he seemed to be getting the hang of it, gave him the thumbs-up. "Check!"

Slater had a plan. He started climbing up the body of the mobster, hand over hand up the chain until he was perched above the corpse. The hook was drifting right, away from the hotel, toward the La Brea Tar Pits, which sat in the middle of the block one street away.

He looked down into a tarry black bubbling pool. The thick, oily liquid was directly below him—and it was the perfect place to deposit Leo, a fitting last resting place, considering the man's nickname in life.

"Danny!" Slater screamed. "Stop the crane! Full stop!"

No problem. On the control panel was a big red button marked: stop. Danny hit it as hard as he could.

When the sound of the crane died away, Slater heard something quite terrifying. Ticking. Leo was ticking. And that couldn't mean anything good.

Frantically, he kicked at the dead mobster, trying to dislodge him, trying to tear the cloth of his suit collar from the thick, blunt iron of the sky hook.

Hanging on with one hand, Slater reached down, his frenzied fingers trying to rip away the piece of material. Evidently, Leo had always bought clothes of a certain quality: the collar refused to give.

Leo was going nowhere, except for the lazy circles he was swinging on the turnbuckle of the hook, his dead, bleached white face leering up at Slater, as if mocking his attempts to kick him clear.

The ticking was louder. Worse than that—it was faster.

"The hell with it!" shouted Slater into the wind. With an angry cry he jumped from his relatively secure perch on the chain, grabbed the corpse of Leo the Fart around the chest in a tight bear hug and added his own dead weight to the *really* dead weight of the body.

But the two combined weights *still* weren't enough to pull Leo free. Slater swung back and forth, like a terrier shaking a rat, desperate to yank the cadaver away from the unforgiving iron of the hook.

"Come on, you gasbag," screamed Slater. *"Come on!"*

As if responding to Slater's angry demand, the cloth gave way, with an abrupt rip that threw both men out into space. Locked together, Slater and Leo plunged toward the tar pit. Head over heels they fell, one of the men alive and kicking, the other dead and ticking.

There was an astonishing splash as they hit the surface of the tar pit, the two bodies throwing up a great plume of black, oily foam. Both sunk beneath the surface, a series of scummy bubbles marking the place where they had hit. It was an impact that would have killed a lesser man than Jack Slater. Lucky for Leo, it was not anything that concerned him now. He sank like a stone, making a beeline for the nether regions of the earth.

The La Brea Tar Pits is one of Los Angeles's best known tourist attractions, and there were a fair number of sightseers standing beside the oil pool when Leo and Jack Slater hit. They could do nothing more than gape, frozen in place.

Slater came blasting straight up out of the ooze, an angry snarl—as well as some tar bubbles—on his lips. The tourists winced.

Jack began to swim strongly for the shore, an even freestyle through the gelatinous goo. He reached the black beach just as Danny came racing in from the construction site. Slater raised his weapon in the air and emptied the magazine.

"Everybody out! *Now,* goddammit!"

He needn't have bothered with the order. Two people dropping into a tar pit—only one of whom emerged—and a deranged pre-teen with a weapon were two things almost guaranteed to empty a tourist attraction.

Slater hauled himself out of the goo pool and waited, Danny at his side. From the Mesozoic depths of the tar pit came an ominous rumbling, a profound visceral gurgling that grew progressively louder.

Danny and Jack watched, horrified, as a giant tar bubble the color of cheap licorice rose from the lake of slime. It was like some resurrected animal struggling to be free. The globule danced on the surface, swelling like Leo in his prime, growing until it was a full ten feet across. Just at the point that it seemed the poison bubble *must* burst, it imploded, gradually growing smaller, subsiding, imprisoned in the tar.

Danny and Slater sighed heavily, relieved that their improvised plan had worked.

"Silent but deadly," breathed Slater.

"Good one," said Danny.

As a service to the visitors of the La Brea Tar Pits, there was a handy dispenser of paper towels not far from where Danny and Jack were standing. Slater grabbed a mammoth handful and started wiping the tar from his face. It came off easily, as if the sticky muck were no harder to budge than a water stain.

Through the layer of paper, Slater rapped out an order: "Bring the car around."

"The helicopter landed on it," said Danny ruefully.

"I hate it when that happens." He had managed to wipe away the sludge, and his face was now clean.

"You know," said Danny sardonically, "tar actually sticks to some people."

"Yeah?" said Slater. "What's your point?"

Just then, Whitney roared into the scene in her giant flame-encrusted Jeep.

"Dad," she said perkily, "I heard you were here, so I figured you could use some clothes. And, of course, if you need some transportation, there's the Jeep."

Danny planted his hands on his hips. Clean clothes, a vehicle . . . This was getting a *little* ridiculous.

"Nobody finds this a little convenient? Nobody here"—he fixed a beady eye on Slater and his daughter—"is bothered by this amazingly inconceivable coincidence?"

Slater grinned. "Kid, all along you've been saying this was a movie." Jack was now completely tar free and dressed in clean clothes. His hair was stylishly mussed, but that was it. The big detective looked as if he had awoken from a good night's sleep and spent an hour at the gym.

"But your other movies at least made some kind of sense. This is going too far."

Jack shrugged. "So this one was probably tampered with by studio executives . . ."

What could Danny say? It made sense.

SIXTEEN

Tony Vivaldi was lazing in his pool, floating on his back, doing his best to quell his growing impatience. He was awaiting the return of Mr. Benedict, eager for his report on the slaughter at Leo the Fart's funeral. He flopped over onto his stomach and swam across the pool to the poolside bar. There he made himself a gaudy tropical drink, complete with a little pink paper umbrella. He slurped the rum noisily and waited, growing more and more peevish with the passing of every long minute.

Finally, Benedict did arrive, approaching silently and appearing by the side of the pool like an apparition. For a moment or two, Vivaldi was unaware his hitman was there. When he finally caught sight of him, he nearly jumped out of his skin.

"Damn near frightened me to death!" the gangster shouted.

"Sorry about that," said Benedict. He had a

funny, rather sinister smile on his face, but Vivaldi figured that was the happy result of being present at a bloodbath.

"So?" Vivaldi demanded. "How did it go? Tell me—I'm dying out here."

"Splendid," said Benedict, an odd confidence in his tone. "It went splendidly."

Vivaldi giggled, delighted. "I want to know it all. Was it perfect? Was it?"

Benedict smiled ironically, like a man who had a piece of information that no one else possessed. "All according to plan. Without a flaw."

"The gas went off okay?" Vivaldi asked eagerly. The plan to wipe out the Torelli family had been his brainstorm, and he was desperately fishing for compliments.

"Like clockwork. You should have seen it. Men, women, and children dropping left and right. Writhing, screaming. Leaping to their doom to escape the pain."

Vivaldi wriggled in the water, in paroxysms of delerious pleasure, as he tried to imagine the scene. "Really?"

"No," said Benedict abruptly. "Not really. I'm lying." He pulled his gun from his belt and pointed it at his esteemed employer.

Vivaldi stopped laughing. "Huh?"

"Everything went to hell," said Benedict, acid in his voice. "In fact, I'm having a terrible day, and it is largely because of you."

Vivaldi didn't understand. "There was no men, women and children leaping to their doom to escape the pain?" He sounded as if he were keenly disappointed.

"No. Nothing like that."

"Benedict, what is this? One minute you're my friend, then the next minute you do a total three sixty on me. What gives with you?"

Benedict's anger reached the flash point. *"One eighty,* you stupid— *One eighty.* If I did a three sixty, I'd go completely around. I'd be back where I started.

Vivaldi didn't seem to get it. "Huh?"

"Oh, what's the use?" Benedict raised his weapon and fired once, the bullet punching a neat little hold in the man's forehead, right at the point where Tony Vivaldi's bushy eyebrows met. Vivaldi looked surprised for a moment, then sank slowly, like an ocean liner going down.

Benedict holstered his gun and walked into the house. "Finally," he said. "No more toadying for second-rate Sicilian thugs. No more fawning for fools who can think of nothing better to do with money than buy bimbos and ludicrous houses." He looked with disgust at the Anglo-Greco-Hispanic architecture of the building.

He drew the ticket out of his pocket and looked at it lovingly. "Now I possess real power. The power to *control.*" His voice grew louder, and a crazy look transformed his face. "If that little turd Daniel Madigan can move through parallel worlds, *I* can move through parallel worlds. In and out." Benedict's fist tightened on the glowing ticket. "In—steal whatever I want—and out. Impossible to catch." He closed his eyes and sighed. "I knew if I said my prayers long enough, someday they would be answered."

"Ahem," said someone behind him.

Benedict whipped around. The tough-looking Asian guy was standing there, dressed in a black suit and a frilly apron. He was trailing a vacuum cleaner behind him like a pull-along toy.

"You want me to vacuum now?" he asked.

"No," said Benedict. "But I suspect the pool could use some attention."

The butler nodded and turned toward the door. He never made it. Suddenly, out of no-where, Whitney's Jeep burst through the wall in a shower of plaster and bricks, the big engine screaming. Slater and Danny jumped from the cab. The Ruger Blackhawk was aimed squarely at Benedict's chest.

"Don't move!" Slater ordered. The butler knew his match when he saw it. He raised his hands.

Benedict hesitated, mulling over the merits of going for his own pistol. He decided against it, choosing life over a heroic moment of blood-shed. Benedict showed his empty hands.

"All right, Slater, I'll go quietly."

Slater holstered the big gun and advanced menacingly. "The hell you will." He slugged Benedict hard in the gut, doubling the villain over.

"That," Slater announced, "was for blowing up my second cousin's house."

Jack seized Benedict by the shoulders and straightened him upright. He raised his hand again, and Benedict winced, anticipating another body-crunching blow. But Slater satisfied himself with a light slap, a meek little tap to the wrist.

"That's for blowing up my ex-wife's house." Then he leaned in, his face dark with anger. "But *this* one is for my daughter's black eye."

Danny had never seen his hero more angry, nor had he seen a more forceful punch. Jack's fist smacked into Benedict's chin, but before he hit the ground, Slater caught him and threw him at the butler. The two of them smashed straight through the wall.

People got thrown through walls all the time in Jack Slater pictures, and they always left a hole at the point of impact. But not this time— Benedict and his Asian pal had disappeared through the wall, as if the barrier had been made of nothing more than Jello.

Danny and Slater stared at the spot. "That doesn't usually happen," said Jack, mystified.

Danny knew exactly what was going on. He thrust his hand into the wall and watched it jiggle and dance as if it were gelatin. Pulling his hand back, he turned to Slater. It was time to face facts, once and for all.

"He has the ticket, Jack. That's the key to everything—it's magic. My world—he's gone over to *my world*." Danny shoved the wall again, and it wiggled under his touch. "The doorway must still be open. Come on. We have to go after him."

Slater looked at the writhing wall, then at Danny; he was hesitating, agonizing about what to do next. "I'm not worried that you're crazy anymore, Danny—I'm worried that you're right."

"I *am* right."

"The problem is . . . if I go, how will I get back?"

"Jack," said Danny angrily, "you can't go through life nitpicking every little thing . . ."

Jack thought for a moment. Then he said: "The hell with it."

Hand in hand, Jack and Danny jumped through the wall and into the real world.

SEVENTEEN

Slater and Danny tumbled through a long, wide corridor of bright white light, falling head over heels toward the real world. They landed with a thud on the dusty carpet of the Pandora Theater. Danny blinked rapidly, staring about him, astonished to see Vivaldi's house on the screen of the movie theater.

"Look," said Danny. "The movie."

But Slater couldn't have cared less. He had caught sight of Benedict and Mr. Chew dashing out of the side door of the theater. Jack hauled Danny to his feet. "Let's go!"

"I oughta see if Nick's okay," Danny stammered.

"There's no time," Slater snapped. "Come on!"

The two of them blasted out of the theater to the street, where Slater came to a skidding stop. He took in the dirty pavement, the smells in the doorways and, eight blocks downtown, the spire of the Empire State Building. Slater looked confused.

"We're in New York?"

"Jack," said Danny, "it all makes sense. I'll explain it to you." He thought for a moment and then shook his head. "No. It makes absolutely no sense, but I'll explain it to you anyway. Later. Meantime, be careful. Things work different here."

Benedict and Mr. Chew had already adapted to their new surroundings. They had flagged down a cab at the corner of Forty-Second Street and Eighth Avenue. The hitman thrust a gun into the cabbie's face.

"Get out!"

This was not the first time the cab driver had found himself in this position. He knew the ropes. "No problem, man," he said, scuttling out of the driver's seat.

Mr. Chew threw himself behind the wheel, and Benedict pulled open the passenger-side door and jumped in.

"Go!"

The cab roared away from the curb just as Jack and Danny turned the corner. There was no doubt in Slater's mind as to what to do next. He unholstered the big Ruger Blackhawk and aimed at the car as it roared up Eighth Avenue.

"Here's another explosion for your movie, kid." The gun bucked and roared, and a bullet hit the body work of the cab. But there was no explosion! In fact, there was no effect at all except a small hole in the trunk. Mr. Chew and Benedict just zoomed away.

Slater went red in the face. He couldn't remember the last time he had fired at a car without blowing it up. He glared at Danny. "Not a word. I don't want to hear one word. Understand?"

"Got it," said Danny.

But Jack couldn't quite seem to give up his movie way of doing things. He pounced on a brand-new Acura Legend parked at the curb and in a second had punched out the window on the driver's side. Unlike in the movies, though, the car did not immediately burst into life without a key, and Slater was forced to squander precious seconds hot-wiring the machine.

Benedict's cab was a good six blocks ahead of them, but Slater, driving fast, came up rapidly. Danny noticed that he seemed distracted, glancing from the road to his right hand.

"What's the matter?"

"My hand . . . it really hurts."

"See," said Danny. "Things work different here. You can't smash a car window with your bare hands and not expect it to hurt."

Slater shot Danny a look. "Thanks for sharing that with me. You couldn't have mentioned this a little earlier?"

"Slipped my mind."

"And another thing, the roads here are terrible." Eighth Avenue was a minefield of ruts, deep potholes and thick bumps of asphalt.

From a movie car chase point of view, the road left a lot to be desired.

"Jack. This is reality. These are real roads."

"Well, they're lousy," Slater grumbled.

"This is the real world. Get used to it." No sooner, though, had the words left Danny's mouth than he had reason to reconsider them.

Up ahead, directly ahead of them, two workmen carried a giant pane of glass across the street; in the middle of the avenue, two workmen sat perched high on ladders, stringing a banner across the street, a brightly colored streamer advertising an upcoming Halloween parade. On the sidewalk, a man tottered from a storefront to his car, staggering under the weight of a towering wedding cake. None of the workmen seemed even remotely concerned that they were working hard at four o'clock in the morning.

Danny gaped. This was the perfect movie comic-relief-in-the-middle-of-tense-car-chase device. It was so much of a cliché that Danny was actually surprised that there was no cart piled high with fruit on the sidewalk. He braced himself for the inevitable impact. If he'd had to guess, he would have said the Acura would smash the glass first, nail the ladders, then ice the cake.

But he had forgotten that this was real life. Despite the fact that the men in the street were prime movie targets, they knew enough to get out of the way as the taxicab and the Acura Legend rocketed by.

"Damn kids!" shouted the guy with the cake. "There oughta be a law!"

But there was some of the magic of the movies at work in the city that night. Following the cab around the corner, Slater suddenly slammed on the brakes and the car slid to a halt. The street was a dead end—Danny couldn't remember ever seeing a dead end street in New York City—and at the far limit of the street sat the taxicab, engine revving.

Slater revved back. Danny groaned. "No. No way. Slater, please, listen to me. It won't work, do you hear me? You can't play chicken in real life. You'll crash!"

But Slater was not to be deterred. "Out of the car, amigo."

Danny was frantic. "This isn't the movies anymore! Here you've gotta reload guns, and car carshes can kill you. You hear me? . . . You. Are. Going. To. *Crash*." He couldn't think of any way of making his words have more impact.

There was the scream of tires burning rubber from the far end of the street. The cab was hurtling toward them.

"Go," ordered Slater, shoving Danny out the door.

"You're gonna die!" Danny screamed as Slater floored it, peeling out.

The two vehicles roared toward each other, racing forward, gaining speed with the passage of each second. The bellowing engines filled the narrow street from wall to wall. The game was called chicken, but it was obvious that the nerve of both drivers was not going to crack. Danny could hardly stand to watch.

The sound of impact was as loud as a bomb. The two cars hit head-on in a metal-shearing fifty-mile-an-hour crash. The glass exploding was as thunderous as a shotgun blast. The two cars locked together and lurched skyward.

Mr. Chew flew through the window of the cab, bounced on the hood of the Acura and crashed through Slater's windshield, showering him with nuggets of shattered glass.

At the instant of impact, Danny was off and running for the terrible crash, fearing for the worst. One look at Mr. Chew's crumpled, broken body told Danny that he had played his last game of chicken. Slater, still alive, sat dazed behind the wheel, stunned by the impact. He was breathing heavily, in pain, the cuts and bruises he had sustained making getting out of the car agony.

"That hurt," he said quietly, still very surprised by what had befallen him.

Danny didn't know whether to be relieved or angry. He chose angry. "You're lucky to be alive, you dumb—"

Slater cut him off. "Eighty-nine Acura Legend," he said. "Standard driver-side air bag." He gestured toward the yellow smoking wreck of Mr. Chew's car. "Checker cab. No air bag." Slater tapped his temple. "So tell me, who's dumb?"

They clambered over the wrecked cab, peering inside. There was no sign of Benedict.

"He couldn't have jumped," said Slater. "Nobody is that good."

"Maybe it was the ticket. Maybe it's on and working all the time now."

Slater just shook his head. His whole world had been turned upside down. He was confused and tired and in pain and wasn't quite sure what to do. However, all of Slater's puzzlement so far was nothing compared to the next real-world shock.

Standing in the middle of Times Square, where Broadway and Seventh Avenue merged, was a giant billboard, a hundred feet high. It was a huge cutout figure: the mammoth version of the standee in the lobby of the Pandora Theater. Slater could only gape, his mouth open.

It was him! The same blue jeans, the same leather jacket, a cigar the size of a station wagon in his giant mouth. In one giant fist he grasped a pump shotgun; in the other, a stick of dynamite.

The figure was wrapped in giant lettering: "Arnold Schwarzenegger is Jack Slater! *Jack Slater IV* Coming Soon to a Theater Near You!"

Danny watched worriedly as reality came crashing in on Jack. His big shoulders slumped; he seemed to be crumbling before Danny's eyes.

"What . . . what is this place?" Jack asked, bewildered. "Where am I now?" He looked

173

questioningly at Danny. "What is happening to me?"

"I tried to tell you," said Danny softly.

Slater's mind whirled. It was all too much for him to take in—it made no sense. What he needed was a cigar. There was a corpse sprawled on a steam grate, and in Slater's experience, corpses always had a cigar tucked away in a pocket. He knelt and started to pat down the body—but the body moved.

"Getthehellouttahere," barked the homeless man. Slater jumped back and stared.

Danny tried to pull him away. "What are you doing?"

"I thought he might have a cigar."

"Jack, you can't do that here."

Slater sighed heavily. "Do you know where I can sit down for a while?" Danny's hero seemed a shadow of his former self.

At three in the morning, New York shows its worst side—and it was a side that fascinated Mr. Benedict. In contrast to Jack Slater, Benedict was quite impressed with the real world—he could detect an undercurrent of sin here that captivated him. He strolled through the darkened streets around Times Square enchanted by the unrelenting tableau of sleaziness. It was the time of night when all the women on the streets look like prostitutes and all the men look guilty of something. Benedict felt right at home—but he was disinclined to make friends.

A haggard-looking hooker staggered out of the shadows and pasted a phoney smile on her face as she lurched toward Mr. Benedict.

"Hey, sweetheart," she said. "How'd you like to have a party? You and me."

Benedict stopped and regarded her critically, as if carefully weighing her words. "Party?" he said. "Certainly. Sex with you? Out of the question."

The hooker looked hurt and flipped him the bird. "Who needs you."

Benedict sauntered on, turning down a side street. Halfway down the block, he stopped, listening as three sharp shots echoed through the night. He peered around a corner, peeking into a shadowy alley.

There were three men in the alley—two alive, one recently dead. The two living, breathing kids looked dispassionately at the corpse sprawled in the dirt.

"Take his shoes," said one.

"Right," said the other, quickly stripping the sneakers from the dead man.

"Steal his shoes?" Benedict was very impressed. In the real world there was such callous disregard for life that people were routinely shot for their *shoes*. Furthermore, no one seemed to think anything about it. No irate bystanders responded to the shots, there was no sound of sirens.

"Now that *is* interesting," he said aloud. Benedict walked on, deep in thought. He strolled a full block before stopping in front of an all-night parking garage. In the glass-fronted office a rent-a-cop dozed fitfully.

Benedict tapped the glass and the security guard awoke with a start.

"What do you want?"

Benedict smiled apologetically. "Sorry. Can you help me?"

The man's eyes narrowed suspiciously. "Depends. What do you need?"

"I was wondering if you'd help me test a theory . . ."

"A theory?"

"Yes." Quickly, Benedict pulled out his pistol, aimed and fired, blasting the poor guy out of his chair. The sound of the shot was as loud as a clap of thunder—surely this would attract attention. Benedict holstered his weapon and waited, just standing there, as if he was waiting for a bus.

Nothing. A subway rumbled by beneath his feet, a ball of dirty newspaper blew down the street, an urban tumbleweed . . . Benedict cleared his throat.

"Ahem . . . Hello!" He filled his lungs and bellowed. "Hello! I've just shot a man! I did it on purpose!" He waited a moment. "I say, I've just murdered a completely innocent man and I wish to confess."

This time there was a response. From out of the darkness somewhere above him came the sound of a window being thrown open.

"Shut up down there!" The voice was irate

and sleepy at the same time. "We're trying to get some sleep!"

The window slammed shut. Benedict smiled and started to walk on. The real world was turning out to be even better than he expected. As he walked, he began to sing, all of the Broadway orchestras in the silent theaters playing in his mind. He started to dance, a spritely little dance with a complicated little back step thrown in.

Benedict gamboled into the night, his heart full of glorious murder. Though, to be fair, it had to be said that for all his faults Mr. Benedict was a very good dancer.

EIGHTEEN

In an all-night New York coffee shop, Benedict and his companion did not stand out at all. With Mr. Chew gone, the hitman had realized he needed some muscle. Using the ticket, he had found the perfect fictional character for the job.

Benedict had bought the bulldog edition of *The New York Times* and was eagerly paging through the movie section.

"This should be fun for you," he said to his new companion. "I realized after the car crash that no matter how often I moved between worlds, I could never rest until I stopped Slater. And *I* can't seem to do it."

Benedict's associate only grunted.

Benedict folded the paper and showed him the full-page ad for the forthcoming Jack Slater movie. "Now, I realize you've never heard of this man, but his name, believe it or not, is Arnold Schwarzenegger."

Benedict's companion studied the picture. "Looks familiar," said The Ripper with a smile. He was caressing something wrapped in brown paper on the coffee table. It was suspiciously axe-shaped.

From the moment he had arrived in the movie world, Danny had longed to tell Nick that the ticket worked. He decided that Jack's intense desire to sit down would have to wait until after they had found Danny's old projectionist friend. He had a feeling he knew exactly where he would be.

Nick was slumped in his chair in the projection booth at the Pandora Theater. He was still wearing his snug uniform, the pillbox hat slightly askew on his head. The old man's mouth was open, and he was snoring faintly.

"Nick! *Nick!*"

The old man awoke with a snort. "Omigod! Danny! I was so worried. I checked on you halfway through the movie, and you were gone!"

"I'm okay. I'm okay. But *you didn't see what happened*?" Danny was incredulous. How could he have missed it?

Nick looked embarrassed. "Aw, kid, I sleep the sleep of the dead in here, you know that. Two in the morning when I woke up, and you weren't here. At first, I thought you'd gone home—but then I figured you wouldn't miss the end of the new Jack Slater. Then I got scared . . ."

"I wasn't home, Nick—I was in the movie. Nick. *The ticket works!*"

Nick paused a moment to digest this bit of startling information.

"I'm getting on in years, Danny," he said finally. "Define 'in the movie' for me."

The definition from Danny's mouth was rather confused, but infectious with excitement as his delerious words tumbled out in a torrent.

"I played chicken against some killers," he babbled breathlessly. "And Whitney kissed me right on the mouth. I drove one of those giant cranes and dropped Leo the Fart into the La Brea Tar Pits." Then, at the top of his voice: "And I was with Jack Slater every step of the way!"

Nick had tears in his eyes—his belief was profound and immediate. "All the years I've wasted . . . been too frightened, but it's not too late . . . I can still go and visit Garbo in *Camille*. Jean Harlow! I had such a crush when I was a young man . . . Monroe in *Bus Stop*."

Nick stopped suddenly and blinked, catching sight of Jack Slater for the first time. "Excuse me for going on like that, sir." He pumped Jack's hand. "I am a great admirer of your work."

"Nick," whispered Danny. "It's not like that. He isn't who you think he is."

But Nick had figured out the situation in an instant. He continued to shake Jack's hand. "This is a wonderful moment for me, Mr. Slater—I've never met a fictional character before. How new and exciting this must be for you."

Slater had gotten over the initial shock, but he still wasn't himself. He felt battered, weary and more than a little confused about this new predicament.

There was nothing thrilling about his situation. "New? Exciting? I just found out I was imaginary." He shook his head sadly. "How would you feel if some Hollywood putz made you up?"

The man had a point. "Not good," said Danny.

"His name is Roger," Slater continued. "He drives an Audi. Your marriage? Your two kids? Nope. Not yours at all. He thought them up too. Good ol' Roger."

"Jack, look on the bright side," said Danny, quickly trying to think of a bright side.

"You *were* supposed to have three kids, but he ran out of typewriter ribbon. And oh, yeah, almost forgot: Roger's throwing your son off a building gives you nightmares, but hell, you're fictional. *So who cares?*" Jack glared at Nick and Danny. "I'm sorry, but I don't find it new and exciting to discover that my life is a god-damn movie."

Nick was moved. He knew what it was like to think that you had lived a wasted life—and he had a profound knowledge of the magic that movies could work. He put an arm around Jack Slater's broad shoulders.

"You're young, you're impressionable, but

listen to me—there are lots worse things than movies. There are politicians and wars and forest fires and famine and sickness and pain and politicians—"

"You said politicians already," said Jack Slater, cutting in.

"I know I did. They're twice as bad as anything."

Slater smiled in spite of his woes. His sour mood was beginning to pass.

But Nick had some bad news of his own. "They've closed the old Pandora, Danny. It's over."

"Closed? When did this happen?"

"Yesterday. I guess I didn't want to tell you until you had seen the last movie ever shown here. I'm all that's left now. I'll be clearing my stuff out, and then it's the wrecking ball . . . but I don't mind. Not now. Now I've got a second chance."

"Second chance? What second chance? Did you get another job?"

"Better than that," said Nick, smiling. He held out his hand. "Can I have my ticket back now?"

A sick little grin appeared on Danny's face. "Um . . . Right. The ticket. Well, you see, Nick, we have this one little hiccup." He swallowed hard, took a deep breath and struggled to break the bad news. "Did you see any of the movie, Nick?"

"I guess I saw the first fifteen minutes or so."

"Do you remember a character called Benedict?"

"The bad guy."

Danny nodded. "That's right. See . . . Benedict is here too, somewhere, and he's got the ticket."

"Benedict?" said Nick, aghast. "The madman with the glass eye? Oh my Lord . . . If he gets into *other* movies, he could bring other people out with him. I sure better hold on to my print of *Jack Slater IV*." Then he looked at Jack Slater with horror in his eyes. "How are *you* going to get back?"

"Don't think I haven't thought about it," grumbled Jack.

Before they could address that question, there was the far more delicate question of getting around Danny's mother. Gingerly, they climbed the stairs to the apartment, moving as quietly as possible.

"Just follow my lead, okay?"

Slater nodded. "Okay."

When Danny slipped his key into the lock, the soft rasp of metal on metal seemed as loud as a plane crash. Both of them froze and listened.

"I think we're okay," Danny whispered.

But they weren't. Suddenly, the door of the apartment swept open and Danny's mother stood there. Jack Slater flattened to the side of the door, as if this were a drug bust. She looked tired and haggard and was still wearing her waitress uniform.

"Hi, Mom," said Danny lamely.

"Don't you 'Hi, Mom' me! Don't you ever do this to me again. Do you know what time it is? It's four in the morning, that's what time it is!"

Like any kid, Danny was embarrassed when his mother got mad at him in front of his friends. He squirmed, humiliated, and tried to quiet her.

"Mom, I'm sorry, okay, sshhh."

Irene Madigan was truly furious. "Don't try and shush me, young man. The police call me at the restaurant, we've been robbed, then you're not here when I get home. What am I supposed to think? There's ninety thousand kids out there with guns, you know!"

"Okay, Mom. I'm fine. Okay—"

"And where have you been? If you've been down at the movie theater with that old lunatic I'll— And get in here. Now." Danny's mom grabbed him by the arm and dragged him into the apartment. Danny pulled back.

"Um, Mom . . . ?"

"I said, get in here!"

"Wait. You know how you always say you wish I had more friends?"

"That has nothing to do with—"

"Wait." He pulled Jack Slater into the doorway. "I want you to meet a new friend of mine."

Irene must have stared for a full minute, her mouth open and her eyes wide. "But," she said finally. "But. You . . . you. You're . . . I

185

mean. Wow!" This reaction was not unexpected. Having a world famous movie star show up on your doorstep at four o'clock in the morning was a little startling.

Jack Slater himself looked a little nonplussed. He held out his hand. "Um . . . hello. Mrs. Madigan, I'm Arnold Braunschweiger."

NINETEEN

Being a character in an action movie was extremely tiring, so when Danny hit the couch that early morning, he fell asleep in an instant, with hardly a moment to consider the wild events of the preceding day and night. He awoke nine hours later, in the middle of a Saturday afternoon. He lay still for a minute or two, not quite sure if his adventures had been nothing more than dreams, the product of an overactive imagination.

Then Danny heard voices coming from the kitchen: his mother's and the unmistakable guttural drawl of the great Jack Slater.

Quickly, Danny pulled on his blue jeans and threw on a shirt and hurried out to the kitchen. Irene Madigan and Jack Slater were sitting at the Formica table, empty coffee cups in front of them. A radio played soft classical music in the background. It was a comfortable, domestic scene—and it was immediately apparent that while Danny had slept, the two adults had become friends.

"Well," said Irene with a smile. "Good morning—good afternoon—to you. Would you like some eggs?"

Danny nodded. "Yeah. Scrambled, please." Then he noticed that his mother was still wearing the same clothes from the night before. "What? Have you been up all night?"

"Why didn't you tell me Jack was a policeman?" Irene Madigan asked. "And that you were looking at mug shots?"

Danny shot a grateful look at Jack—it looked as if he had gotten him off the hook with his mom. Of course, he should have expected no less. That was what partners did: they covered for each other in the face of a greater authority, like chiefs of police, political figures and irate mothers.

But Jack did not look happy. "And why didn't you tell me you didn't have any friends?" Jack demanded. "And what's this business going to the movies at midnight when you knew your mother would be worried?"

Irene glanced at her son, a triumphant smile on her lips. Danny realized that given the choice, adults would always stick together.

"Mom," said Danny, "you've turned him into a wimp."

Danny's mother shook her head. "He's just more three-dimensional, that's all. Toast?"

"No, thanks." Danny had no interest in toast whatsoever. He was far more concerned about

188

his hero. While Mrs. Madigan bustled about getting breakfast, Danny whispered, "Jack, are you okay?"

Slater looked very puzzled. "We talked. I've never just . . . talked . . . to a . . . woman."

Danny squinted at him and muttered under his breath: "Wimp. Next they'll be doing that *mushy* stuff." Right now, the most important thing was to bring Jack back up to hero mode and quickly.

"Me and Jack are going out today," Danny announced. "I'm helping him. On a case."

Danny's mother frowned. "Your license to kill has been grounded, young man," she said sternly.

"Mom," Danny protested. "I *have* to help. I'm a witness."

But as far as Irene Madigan was concerned, the storm from Danny's shenanigans of the night before had not yet blown over. "You'll need a witness! I get off the night shift at four in the morning and you're not home? What are you trying to do? Kill me?"

Slater tried to intercede for Danny. "Irene . . . There's nothing to worry about."

Danny's eyebrows shot up. *Irene.* Things were worse than he had thought. The next thing you knew, Slater wouldn't be loaning him a gun anymore.

"Don't worry," said Jack. "It won't be hard. There are only eight million people in this city . . . And I'm very good at catching people."

"Yeah," said Danny brightly. "And the future of the world may be at stake! And maybe—"

"Wait." Jack Slater held up a hand. He was listening intently to the music coming from the radio, a light and sparkling piece of classical piano. "Could you turn that up, please?"

It was a sprightly, uplifting piece, simple and beautiful. The hard planes of Slater's face softened as he listened, a slightly goofy smile on his face.

"What is that?" he asked, his voice hushed.

"That's Mozart," said Irene.

"The guy Practice killed?" Slater asked Danny.

It was actually the andante from Mozart's Piano Concerto Number 21 in C Major, K.467— better known as the theme from the movie *Elvira Madigan.*

For a moment, Danny was about to explain about the movie *Amadeus,* but then he thought better of it. "That's right, Jack. Same guy."

The music moved Slater more than he cared to admit. "It's pretty."

"You like classical music?" asked Danny's mom. As far as she knew, policemen did not have a highly developed sense of the aesthetic.

Slater shook his head. "I don't know . . ." He listened to the airy piano and the delicate strings a little longer. "Yeah. I think I will."

Danny rolled his eyes. *Oh boy*. What Jack needed was a little action. "We gotta get you outta here."

• • •

From the observation deck of the Empire State Building, the city of New York looked vast, imposing and completely overwhelming. From the one hundred and second story, the city stretching to the far horizon, it became apparent to Danny just how difficult it would be to find one man in that huge, roiling mass of humanity. Real life was considerably different from the movies.

Danny stared down at the thousands of pedestrians on Thirty-Fourth Street and shook his head.

"Did you tell my mom who you really are?"

Slater nodded. "Yeah. I told her I was a cop from LA."

"I mean *really*."

"That's real enough . . . for now."

Danny looked north to the great thicket of skyscrapers in midtown. "You really expect to catch him?"

Slater looked down. "I always catch everybody."

Danny looked skeptical. "Yeah? What are you going to do? Spot him from up here?"

Slater gave his diminutive sidekick one of those "oh, ye of little faith" looks. "Look—you're from Pennsylvania; I've never been anywhere real. I'm getting my bearings, that's all. Where are most of the movie theaters?"

Danny pointed to the middle west side. "Over there."

"C'mon, we'll concentrate on that area."

As they strode across town, Slater stared

about himself wide-eyed. He knew New York from its movie reputation, but not even that low status had prepared him for just how, well, strange it was. The crowds on Broadway looked more or less like crowds everywhere, men and women hurrying, going about their business in the big city—except that mixed in with that throng were bizarrely dressed people. Characters dressed up like clowns and goblins and gorillas and transvestites and—this was the really strange part—*no one seemed to notice or care*.

Danny looked completely unconcerned as people as grotesque as odd marine life floated by him on the street.

"Uh, Danny . . ."

"Yeah?"

"Do you notice anything . . . uh, strange?"

Danny's head whipped around as twelve people dressed as a dozen identical slices of pizza walked by. "No. You?"

"Well . . ." He gestured toward a trio of kids dressed up like members of the British royal family coming toward them.

"Oh," said Danny with a grin. "I get it. That's for Halloween. There's a big parade every year. On Sixth Avenue. It goes on all night."

"I see," said Slater. Then he stopped. "Look."

Danny looked. A man dressed as a nun was standing on a street corner lighting a cigarette and waiting for the light to change. "Jack. It's not a real nun. It's a costume."

"No. Not him. Beyond him." Slater pointed. "That store there."

Danny looked. It was a small storefront so heavily defended with gratings and metal bars that it took a moment to figure out the sign stenciled in the window. "Guns. Ammo. Police Equipment," Danny read. "Yeah? So?"

"This where we wait for Benedict," said Slater unequivocally. He stopped and ducked into a doorway, keeping the gun shop in plain sight.

It was beginning to drizzle, and Danny flipped up his collar. "Here? Why? You expect Benedict is going to show up here and just tap us on the shoulder? Is that your plan?" The tone of Danny's voice suggested that he didn't think much of Slater's plan if that was all there was to it.

"Probably not," said Jack with a shake of his head. "But he must know that my gun doesn't work as well here. Maybe he figured out his doesn't work so hot either. He might try trading up."

It was, Danny thought, about the flimsiest scheme he had ever heard. Even in magic-of-the-movies terms it was pretty thin. But Jack Slater looked unconcerned; in fact, he looked as if he weren't thinking about it at all. He was staring into the window of the store next to the gun shop. It was a florist shop, and he seemed lost in the profusion of blooms in the display case.

"The flowers are very beautiful," he said reverently.

"Yeah," said Danny. "They're great." This was not the Jack Slater he knew and loved.

His reverie was interrupted. A kid no older than Danny and dressed in a skeleton costume stopped dead in the middle of the street and gaped at Slater.

"Omigod," the kid gasped, awestruck. "It's Arnold."

"Beat it," growled Slater.

"Jack," Danny whispered, "kids here . . . they idolize you."

Jack figured he couldn't disappoint his public. "Sorry," he said to the kid/skeleton.

"That's okay." He gave a thumbs-up. "*Total Recall* was awesome."

Slater looked questioningly at Danny. "*Total Recall*?"

"Secret agent on Mars," he stage-whispered.

"Right. Thanks."

"Keep up the good work, Arnold."

"I'll do my best." He grabbed Danny. "This isn't working. Let's get out of here."

"Now where?"

"Glass eyes."

"Good thinking."

There was nothing in the New York Telephone Yellow Pages under "Glass Eyes," nor was there anything under "Prosthetics—Optical," but they hit pay dirt under the heading of "Artificial Eyes—Human." In fact, they hit a little too much pay dirt—there was half a page of places in New York City that sold glass eyes. Danny and Jack Slater were impressed.

"I didn't think there would be all that much call for them," said Slater.

"I guess it's a New York kind of thing," said Danny. Finally, they chose the one that happened to be closest to Times Square and the theater district. The glass-eye shop they picked had the added advantage of being right next door to an art shop that specialized in cheap reproductions of popular paintings. While Danny watched the glass-eye shop, Slater continued his education in the beauties of the real world, intently studying pictures by some of the French Impressionists, notably Monet, Renoir and Cézanne.

Danny was getting decidedly antsy. He was also getting wet, the drizzle having turned to steady rain. "I thought we were supposed to look for him, find him and finish him."

Slater reluctantly tore his eyes away from one of Monet's studies of Rouen Cathedral. "In my world, they leave clues . . . If I can't find them, they show up and kidnap me. Don't worry." He held up two fingers pressed tightly together. "I'm this far from capturing him."

"I hope so . . ."

Another wave of kids dressed for Halloween was blowing down the street. In a matter of seconds, Jack Slater was surrounded by a Terminator, a Commando and an Teenage Mutant Ninja Turtle.

"I loved *Predator*," said the Commando.

Slater looked to Danny. *"Predator?"*

"Alien in the jungle," he said.

"Alien in the jungle? That sounds terrible!"

"Not so terrible. They made a sequel."

"They did? Was I in it?"

"No."

"Good career move," said Slater.

TWENTY

It was Danny's first real day of genuine police work, and as the cold, wet hours passed, he learned a valuable and genuine fact about the life of a detective. It was *boring*.

Standing about on a chilly, rain-slick sidewalk was not his idea of an action-hero type activity. His mind wandered back to just yesterday, when the bad guys showed up on cue and buildings blew up with a satisfying regularity. All Danny had had since arriving in the real world was a single lousy car chase and a game of chicken, not to mention a severe talking to from his mother. So lost was he in his daydreams that he almost failed to notice Benedict coming out of the glass-eye shop.

Danny caught sight of their nemesis slipping into a taxicab just north of Times Square. Almost immediately the yellow car vanished into a sea of similar vehicles on Seventh Avenue. Hysterical, he tugged at Slater's sleeve. "Jack! There he is! It's Benedict."

"Where?"

Danny pointed into the knot of taxicabs. Suddenly the enchantment of sweet music, the beauty of flowers and the arresting charm of great art vanished from Jack Slater's brain. He got that "I'm gonna get you" stone-cold look on his face—his movie face—and he waded into the maelstrom of midtown rush-hour-in-the-rain traffic.

For Jack Slater, there was only one way to get through a automotive blizzard like that. He clambered up onto the cab closest to him and marched along a thoroughfare of yellow metal, roof to roof. The drivers blasted him with their horns as if they were machine guns and hollered at him in a dozen different languages. If you had been listening very closely, you would have learned how to say "Who is that large maniac on the roof of my cab?" in Urdu, Farzi, Ukrainian, Russian, Spanish, Hindi and a good fifteen American dialects, including Aspiring Actor.

Danny watched with tears of pride in his eyes. *This* was the Jack Slater he knew, this was the man who always won, mowed down the bad guys and saved the girl. Benedict was seated in his cab, calmly reading his newspaper and blissfully oblivious to the avenging movie good guy bearing down on him.

All Danny could do was beam. In that moment, Jack Slater was the most mighty man in the city. He was the punishing angel, his fiery sword replaced by the thundering Ruger Blackhawk. He was all-powerful, vulnerable to nothing—except a slippery cab roof. One cab away from Benedict, Jack Slater missed his footing and teetered for a moment on the edge, fighting to regain his balance. But he couldn't. He tumbled to the wet street, into the path of an onrushing cab.

The taxi slammed on its brakes, but it slipped on the slick surface, the edge of the bumper catching Slater and tossing him six feet.

"Jack!" shrieked Danny. In a second, he was off and running into traffic.

If they had been listening closely this time, Jack and Danny would have learned many colorful phrases in Cantonese.

Slater managed to stagger to his feet just as Danny reached him. "Jack! Jack! Are you all right?"

"Yeah. Yeah . . ." Jack Slater muttered. This real-world stuff was a lot harder—and more painful—than he had anticipated. It made him all the more determined to get Benedict and get him but good.

"C'mon." Slater threw himself on Benedict's cab and tore open the door so hard for a moment it seemed that he would tear it from its hinges.

"No! No!" protested the driver. "Off duty! Off duty!"

But it was empty. Slater had caused enough

commotion for their archenemy to realize what was going on and make his escape. All that remained was Benedict's crumpled newspaper.

Slater slammed his fist onto the roof of the cab. "I don't believe it! Damn!" He strode back toward the sidewalk.

Danny trailed behind him, holding Benedict's newspaper. He thrust it under Slater's nose. "Jack! Look at this!"

The paper was open to the movie page. A big ad had been circled, and Slater could only stare as he tried to make sense of the words. But there it was, in bold black letters: "TONIGHT: IN PERSON. ARNOLD SCHWARZENEGGER IN THE WORLD PREMIERE OF *JACK SLATER IV*."

TWENTY-ONE

Despite the rain, crowds had begun gathering outside of the Radio City Music Hall long before the premiere of the new Jack Slater movie was due to kick off. Among the throng huddled along busy Sixth Avenue and flanking Fiftieth Street were Danny and Jack Slater, a baseball cap pulled down almost to his ears. The last thing he needed was to be harassed by curious, awestruck Schwarzenegger fans. He did attract some curious glances, but with Halloween going on, people just figured that he was another Arnold wannabe, with exceptional makeup skills.

"Shouldn't we be inside?" Danny whispered.

"Benedict wants me," said Slater. "Where I am is what matters. He's a shooter. We watch the rooftops and work the crowd. And *I* stay in the open."

The crowd had forgotten Jack by the time the real Arnold Schwarzenegger showed up, his huge limousine pulling up in front of the theater to be greeted by a dazzling barrage of popping flashbulbs.

The second the master of ceremonies caught sight of the mammoth superstar stepping from his limo, he snatched up his microphone and fought his way through the crowd of reporters and photographers to the red carpet that led into the lobby of the theater.

The applause, the cameras, the shouts of photographers quickly reduced the crowd scene to deafening bedlam, the voice of the MC rising above the din.

"Yes, ladies and gentlemen, Mr. Arnold Schwarzenegger with his lovely and talented wife, Maria Shriver!"

Danny glanced anxiously at Slater when Schwarzenegger stepped into view of the crowd and waved to his fans. There was a dark and brooding look on Jack's face, as if until that moment he hadn't really believed that he was a fictional character, brought to life by the flesh-and-blood man across the street.

In addition to that, there was a persistent aching in his shoulder from getting smacked by the cab, and he had been standing in the chilly rain for several hours. He hurt, he was tired, he was cold, and he had no identity of his own. All in all, not a red-letter day for the fictional Jack Slater.

The master of ceremonies was doing his best to corral the celebrities for a quick pre-

premiere interview. Mrs. Schwarzenegger had some last minute advice for her husband.

"Please—don't plug the restaurants. I *hate* it when you plug the restaurants. Or the gyms. It's so tacky. It's humiliating." The ability to smile and whisper at the same time was one of the hallmarks of true celebrity, and Maria Shriver was a master of the art.

The master of ceremonies thrust the microphone into Arnold's face.

"Tell us about *Jack Slater IV,* Arnold," he said unctuously. "I know you're proud of it, but how is it different from the first three?"

Arnold flashed his movie-star smile. "It's night and day. This one goes much deeper. It has many more philosophical implications, a much more religious aspect. We only kill twenty-two people in this one compared to an average of over sixty in the others."

"That's great, Arnold."

Schwarzenegger nodded. "That's true. Deeper, deeper, deeper. That's my motto."

"And what can we look for next?" The MC was already scanning the crowd for what he was going to do next. The length of a celebrity interview was usually measured in seconds, and he had to spot the next famous face in the crowd.

"My next movie is a biography of Sigmund Freud. I wrote the screenplay myself. Playing a tiny psychiatrist will be an acting stretch for me, I know, but if you keep repeating yourself, the audience finds you out. However"—and here he paused as if about to impart a piece of little-known information—"Freud was Austrian too, you know. For once, no accent problems."

The master of ceremonies started to clap. "Just a wonderful Hollywood success story."

Arnold nodded and saw his opening. "Yes. And speaking of Hollywood—"

But he wouldn't get in any plugs that time. Maria Shriver tugged him away from the mike. She did her smiling and whispering at the same time routine. "You're just hopeless," she hissed. "You shouldn't play a tiny psychiatrist, you should try seeing one."

The master of ceremonies had found his next celebrity. Strolling down the red carpet was a very big, rather ugly man. He was dressed in scarecrow tatters and was carrying a very large, very sharp axe.

"Oh dear! Look who's turned up to celebrate. It's The Ripper from *Jack Slater III*. Scary! Let's *axe* him a question, shall we?" Two thirds of the audience rolled their eyes.

The Ripper stopped dead in his tracks, fear in his eyes. He had never been confronted with a posse of entertainment photographers and an oily MC before. The mike was right under his nose.

"Hello, Rip, what are you up to tonight?"

The commotion and flashbulbs made his speech impediment far worse.

"I-I-I thought I might kill someone," he managed to stammer.

The MC laughed good-naturedly and patted The Ripper on the back. "How about that, folks? What a cutup!" He had already lost interest in The Ripper and his lame jokes. "Look, folks! It's Jamie Farr!"

The Ripper's less than fifteen minutes of fame had come to an end. He wandered toward the main door of the theater and was about to enter when a security guard stopped him.

"I'm sorry, sir. I can't let you in dressed like that. My instructions are to admit guests in black tie only."

The Ripper glared at the rent-a-cop and fingered the axe, itching to use it on this self-important pip-squeak. His instructions were to get into the theater, and he would use any means necessary to carry out his orders. But before he could shed any blood, an immaculately dressed man, his black tie hidden under a perfect camel's hair overcoat, rushed up and got between The Ripper and his would-be victim.

"It's okay, Officer. This man is an actor. I'm his agent. I'll clear this whole thing up." Before the security guard could reply, the agent shoved The Ripper through the big doors and into the lobby.

"What are you doing?" The Ripper demanded.

"Jesus H. Christ, Brad, are you nuts? You wanna play axe murderers for the rest of your life? Come on, let's get you cleaned up." The agent waved a fifty-dollar bill under the nose of the nearest usher. "I need to use the manager's office for five minutes . . ."

The agent hustled the man he thought was his client into the office and snatched up the phone, dialing fast. "Save me from method actors," he muttered as he listened to the phone ring. "Yeah. Marty. I need a tux as fast as you can get it to me. What? What do you mean you can't?"

The Ripper had figured out that he was improperly dressed. The man on the phone had a nice overcoat that would cover his rags. He stole up behind the agent and raised his axe . . .

No one in the line to get into the movie noticed the tall man with a wild look in his eyes and a bloody axe stuffed under his faultless tan overcoat.

The MC was still out front harvesting celebrities. A handsome young man in a perfect tuxedo was smiling broadly as he made his way up the red carpet.

"And here's a late arrival," the master of ceremonies crowed. "Ah yes, it's Brad Conners, the actor who played The Ripper in *Jack Slater*—" A look of profound puzzlement crossed his face, and he glanced at the main door of the theater. "But I thought . . ."

Things seemed to be slightly out of control. The crowd had grown beyond manageable size and seemed a little out of hand. Danny was buffeted by the horde, like a small boy swamped by a strong tide. It seemed too much to expect that they could find Benedict in this throng. In the real world, Jack Slater couldn't see all and know everything. Benedict could slip by unnoticed.

Danny tugged at Jack's sleeve. "I'm getting scared, Jack," he said.

"Don't be," said Slater. "Benedict is afraid of me. I've seen it in his eyes. He knows he cannot stop me."

That didn't make Danny feel any better because, in that moment, a truly horrible thought crossed his mind. Horrible and obvious. Why hadn't they seen it before?

"Jack! He can't stop you but . . . what happens if he's here to stop *him*?"

"Him?"

"Schwarzenegger!"

Slater thought for a second as the full implication of Danny's words sunk in. Then he was off and running for the main door of the theater, waving a police badge at the cop on the door.

"I thought Dekker took that from you," said Danny.

"He took mine. This belongs to someone else." He flipped the leather wallet open: Federal Bureau of Investigation.

"Practice's?"

"That's right. I stole it from him."

Danny could only shake his head in admiration for his hero. That was really thinking ahead.

Jack tore the baseball cap from his head and pounced on the nearest usher. Now he *wanted* to be mistaken for the superstar himself.

"Where am I sitting?" he demanded of the usher. The poor young woman was a little taken aback at the sudden demand from a man who was soaking wet and poorly dressed, but undeniably the celebrity himself.

"Where?"

She trembled as she pointed to the wide, elegant staircase. "Um . . . there are two balconies. I think you're in the lower one."

"Thanks." Slater spun on his heel and grabbed Danny by both shoulders. "You stay."

Danny nodded, resigned to his sidekick role. "Yeah, I know. I stay here."

"And be careful," cautioned Slater. Before Danny could reply, Slater was pushing his way up the stairs, elbowing aside the guests filing into the theater. Jack was aware that he was being rude—and that he wasn't doing Schwarzenegger's reputation any good at all.

TWENTY-TWO

Sidekickdom came easy to Danny, so he knew exactly what role he had to play. He paced nervously in the lobby of the theater, pausing every few steps to listen for sounds of gunshots, screams—some kind of mayhem from the auditorium. But there was no sound more alarming than the busy hum of a thousand people waiting for a movie to begin. But Danny knew better.

"I should be checking the other balcony," he said aloud, psyching himself up. "Definitely."

That was just about all the encouragement he needed. Danny darted into the crowd, a small boy wriggling between the larger people like a fish. But even he could only travel so far in the press of eager moviegoers, and when traffic got tight, Danny found himself stuck.

He craned his neck and looked forward, hoping to catch a glimpse of Jack or Benedict, but instead he saw something that made his blood run cold: a tall man in a tan overcoat who looked familiar. The Ripper seemed to feel Danny's eyes on him. He turned. He saw Danny and smiled. It was not a friendly smile.

Danny snapped his face away, praying that he hadn't been seen. Frustration bubbled up. He was inches away from a child murderer with an axe, and there was absolutely nothing he could do about it. Except one thing. Danny filled his lungs and yelled.

The first person Jack Slater had seen on entering the theater was Schwarzenegger, seated in the front row of the lower balcony. Seeing him up close like this was mesmerizing, as if he were looking at a smoother, sleeker version of himself. The star was dressed in faultless evening clothes, his wife a picture of elegance. Slater could only stare at this man, his alter ego from another world.

"I'll be a son of a bitch," he whispered. Then he heard Danny's voice, loud and scared, high up in the heavens of the giant theater.

"Jack! It's the Ripper! Benedict has brought back The Ripper!"

Slater careened to the front of the balcony and stared up, and there, in the upper tier, was The Ripper, a reincarnated nightmare from his past. For an instant, the two archenemies locked eyes, the two men lost together in time and space. Then The Ripper raised his axe, ready to throw.

In a split second, the Ruger appeared in

Slater's hand and he was crouched in a firing stance.

"Everybody down!" he bellowed. "Down! Now!"

Needless to say, the crowd, completely spooked, did exactly the opposite. People were on their feet, shouting and screaming in blind panic. Slater tried to shut out the chaos and drew a bead on the tan coat as The Ripper dashed across the upper balcony, toward the boxes that flanked the stage.

For a moment, Slater had his nemesis square in his sights, a nice clear bull's-eye. One shot and it was all over. Jack's finger tightened on the trigger . . .

Then he was hit from behind, a heavyweight tackle with enough force behind it to throw the gun from his hands. Slater looked over his shoulder. Schwarzenegger himself had brought him down.

"Get off me, you jackass!"

Schwarzenegger stared at him, not quite able to believe his eyes.

Slater scowled at him. "Yeah, yeah. I look like you. I know. Now, get off me."

Schwarzenegger got to his feet, brushing dust from his black tie. "The studio should tell me when they're planning a stunt," he said. He was still staring intently at Jack Slater. "You know, you are definitely the best celebrity look-alike I've ever seen . . ."

Slater wasn't interested. He grabbed the gun and started up the aisle, searching for Danny, but Arnold hung on with him, friendly now. "I have to say, there's one guy in Idaho who is better than you, in the face mainly, but you are really good."

"That's great," growled Jack Slater.

"Call my office the next time you're in LA," said Arnold affably. "I can get you lots of work—birthday parties, bachelor dinners. The money really adds up, you know."

Slater was scanning the crowd. The Ripper had vanished and so had Danny.

"Are you in a union? SAG? AFTRA?"

Jack turned angrily on Schwarzenegger. "Look—I don't really like you, all right? You've brought me nothing but pain."

"Me?" said Arnold, genuinely aggrieved. "What have *I* ever done to you?"

Jack had no time to argue. The Ripper was loose somewhere in the building, and there was no sign of Danny. The crowd was completely spooked, and he had offended the world's number one box-office star. *Another* completely lousy day in the real world.

And it was about to get worse.

From somewhere in the roiling crowd came a high-pitched, blood-curdling scream. Jack Slater knew that voice: it was Danny's.

Slater accelerated, thundering through the crowd like a linebacker, drilling a hole in the mass of bodies between him and the exit. He blasted into the lobby and out into the rain-swept streets. The afternoon drizzle had intensified into a full-fledged storm; the sky was alive with blasting thunder and crackling lightning . . . as dramatic as a tempest in a movie. A wicked wind whipped at him, as rain pelted the glass of the box office, almost obliterating a message that had been scrawled there in blood. It read: "Slater. The roof."

TWENTY-THREE

Jack Slater exploded onto the roof, his Ruger at the ready, but the scene was all too familiar. The Ripper stood at the edge of the roof, the blade of the axe pressed against Danny's throat.

The fiend had to shout to make himself heard above the vicious storm. "Welcome, old friend!" he said with a sneer. "I had a feeling you would come."

Slater was frozen in place, his face as cold and as hard as a block of stone. It was his old nightmare, only this time it was no movie, this was life or death. It was actually happening, with a genuine flesh-and-blood child here in the real world. Danny was terrified, his eyes wide.

"Are you okay, Danny?"

Danny did his best to be brave. "Y-yes, sir . . ."

"Get rid of the gun, Jack," The Ripper ordered. "I'll kill the boy."

Jack hesitated for a moment. The last time he had thrown away his gun, catastrophe had enveloped him and his son.

"I said, get rid of the goddamn gun, Jack!" The axe blade tightened on Danny's throat.

There was pain in Jack's face, and his white-hot anger threatened to overwhelm him. It took all of his self-control to force himself to give up the gun. He tossed it out into the wind and rain, and it flew over the edge of the roof.

"There," he said. "The gun is gone. It's between you and me now. Let the boy go."

The Ripper chuckled. "We've played this number before, haven't we, Jack?" He scratched his chin with the edge of the axe blade. He seemed, for a second or two, to be deep in thought. "Now let's see, what comes next? You throw away the gun, we did that part already . . . You tell me to let the boy go . . . Done that." Then The Ripper shrugged. "Ah, the hell with it. I'm getting bored. Let's just skip to the end."

"The end?"

"You remember, Jack. This part." The Ripper lifted Danny off his feet, and casually, tossed him off the roof, out into the void. Danny shrieked and then fell from sight.

Jack Slater's mouth dropped open. In all his years of fighting movie bad guys never —*never*—had he seen such a callous, cold-hearted murder. And to crown it all, The Ripper was laughing. *Laughing!*

"That's called revenge, Jack," he said between giggles. "Feels good. I recommend it."

216

Slater was trembling with anger, and for a moment he was not sure he would be able to speak. The words came out of him strangled and choked. "That was . . . a mistake."

"A mistake? No. No mistake." The Ripper lifted the axe. "That was only part one, Jack. Here's part two."

The axe whistled through the air, straight for Jack's head. Slater flung himself aside, the blade sailing by him and embedding itself in a wooden power pole.

Jack didn't miss a beat. He yanked the axe free and swung it, slicing into the power line that snaked up the side of the pole. The cable fell, hissing and spitting sparks on the wet roof top just as Slater launched himself at the pole, pulling his feet up tight under him.

The roof came alive with the millions of volts of raw electricity that powered the entire huge theater, each puddle crackling. The voltage flooded into The Ripper, and he danced and skittered as if on a hot griddle, as every nerve and muscle in his body burned out. Behind him, an entire city block blacked out, The Ripper's dying scream wailing out of the darkness.

"I'll be baaaaaack!"

The current had shut off, and Slater dropped back down to the rooftop and stood over the smoking, scorched body of his latest kill. He felt no elation, no satisfying revenge. He felt nothing but sadness.

"I'll be waiting," he said.

Then, above the crashing of the storm, he heard something that galvanized him. A voice. A very tiny, very scared little boy's voice.

"Jack," Danny squeaked. "Help."

Slater threw himself to the side of the building and saw Danny. He was twenty feet down, just hanging onto the snout of a stone gargoyle. Beneath him were twenty stories of the void, an ocean of open, black air.

"Hang on! I'll be right there!" Slater didn't think—he reacted, throwing himself over the side, clambering down the slippery bricks like a spider, supremely confident. He felt for grips and toeholds . . . except, this was reality. There weren't any. Slater felt himself sliding down the slick side, frantically grabbing for something, *anything* that could arrest his fall. His fingers grabbed a handful of brick. His face slammed against the wall, and he was breathing hard. His feet were dangling out in the abyss.

"Danny?" Slater gasped. "This is really, really hard."

"Tell me about it! Please hurry!"

"Hang on. I'm finishing a magazine. *Of course I'll hurry*." He managed to crane his head over his shoulder to look down into the void, terrified by the wind and the rain-whipped darkness. Jack Slater closed his eyes. "God, please . . ." he implored. "*Please* don't let him die."

Painfully, slowly, Slater managed to crawl a

few feet until he was hanging, one-handed, just above Danny. He reached down . . .

"Okay kid, plan A. You grab my hand and we get out of here."

"That's your plan?" Danny shouted.

"Plan A, yes."

"What's plan B?"

"We fall twenty stories."

Danny shot him a disgusted look. "That's really great, Jack. Really using the old head."

"It's not a great plan," said Slater. "I'll grant you that." He stretched his arm to its limits. "Come on, grab my hand."

"Jack," Danny cried, "you can't support both our weights. We'll fall!"

Slater sighed heavily. "Danny, you can't go through life nit-picking about every little thing . . ."

There really was nothing else to be done. Danny swallowed hard and reached out, trembling, for Jack. His tiny hand disappeared into Slater's big fist, and he let go of the gargoyle. Slater grunted and took the weight, his face a mask of pain mixed with determination, his tendons bunched like steel cable. His arm retracted like a hydraulic lift, dragging Danny toward the edge of the roof and safety.

"Jack . . ." Danny gasped. "What you're doing . . . it's not possible."

"You're right. Now, shut up while I do it."

Slater's teeth were embedded in his lower lip, his eyes were closed tight, as if he were concentrating on gathering up every ounce of strength in his body and willing it into his tensed right arm.

With a roar like a weight lifter, Slater flexed his arm and threw Danny up onto the roof, landing him square in a puddle. Danny rolled onto his back, gasping for breath as Slater hauled himself to safety. Jack collapsed. He was bruised, beaten and bloody, but he was triumphant.

"This hero stuff has its limits," he panted. He rubbed his shoulder and winced in pain. "Now, get me to a hospital. My shoulder is out of the socket." Danny struggled to his feet.

Out of the wind and the darkness came a voice. Benedict's voice. "A hospital, Jack? Will a morgue suffice?"

TWENTY-FOUR

The ubiquitous Mr. Benedict lolled against the stairway door, his hand full of gun, and without further ado, he fired.

"Danny, down." Slater slapped Danny's legs out from under him, throwing him out of the line of fire. Together, they slithered across the rain slick roof, grabbing for the only cover available, the low brick wall of the elevator housing. Jack and Danny crouched behind the barrier, unarmed and helpless. Slater rubbed his throbbing shoulder, trying to quiet the pain.

"Give it up, Benedict," Jack yelled. "The lobby is swarming with cops."

Benedict sniggered. "And that is precisely why I'll avoid the lobby. And if I should, by chance, encounter any law enforcement personnel"—he tapped his glass eye—"I've another explosive surprise for them." Then, casually, he walked toward them, his gun spitting bullets.

The big slugs chewed a piece out of their cover. "Gentlemen," Benedict said, his voice dripping with irony, "as you are about to die anyway, I might as well tell you the entire plot."

"Once a fictional character," said Danny in disgust, "always a fictional character."

Benedict chortled and fished the ticket stub out of his pocket and gazed at it, madness in his eyes. "Think of the villains, Jack. Go ahead. It's easy. You want Dracula? Hang on, I'll fetch him. Dracula? Hell, I'll get *King Kong*."

"Kong was misunderstood," whispered Danny. Benedict fired again. Danny and Jack both winced as another round blew out some more of their cover.

"I'll dine with Freddy Krueger, shop for chainsaws with Leatherface. Plan a party for Hitler. Why not? I'll invite Dr. No and Hannibal Lechter, and we'll all have a christening for Rosemary's baby. Think of the *villains*, Jack." Benedict seemed genuinely entranced with his enthralling vision of cinematic evil.

As if to punctuate his words, he pulled the trigger again, and a hot round ricocheted out into the night. "All I need do is snap my fingers and they'll come, oh yes . . . They're lining up to get here. And do you know why, Jack? Because here in the real world, Jack, the *bad guys can win*." Benedict was standing directly over Slater now, the gun leveled at his head. He spoke with sincere regret. "I'll miss you, Jack," he said. Then he pulled the trigger.

The gun went "click."

Benedict gaped at the revolver. "Click?" he yelled at the weapon. "What's that supposed to mean? Click?"

Jack Slater rose, smiling through his pain. "Gee," he said, "did you make a movie mistake?" He shook his head slowly, as if sympathizing with the movie villain. "Reality is a bitch, pal, you forgot to reload the damn gun . . . Almost had me."

The look of dumbfounded amazement on Benedict's face vanished, to be replaced with his usual smarmy sneer. "Sorry, Jack. I still have you. I just left one chamber empty." *Then* he fired.

The bullet slammed into Slater's chest, the force of impact picking him up and throwing him back. Then he tumbled to the ground, hitting the roof like a felled redwood.

Danny's eyes were wide, almost bulging out of his head. Jack Slater, his hero, was sprawled spread-eagled in a pool of blood-tinged rainwater.

"Jack . . ." whimpered Danny.

Slater opened his mouth and tried to speak, but all he could do was cough blood. He shook his head slowly . . . sadly . . . the light in his eyes fading . . .

Benedict looked vastly pleased with his handiwork. "So sad," he said.

That was all it took. Danny completely flipped out, diving for Benedict with all the power his small body could muster. He was using everything he had to hurt his enemy—kicking, nails scraping, fists flying. "You son of a bitch!"

But Danny couldn't hope to prevail against a strong, grown man. Disdainfully but viciously, Benedict swatted him across the face, throwing him to the bricks. The boy hit the wall hard.

Danny looked up, holding his limp right arm in his left hand. He stared at his damaged limb. "My arm!" he wailed. "You broke my arm. *You broke my arm!*" Suddenly, he was choking on his sobs, bawling like a baby.

Benedict ignored him, turning on Slater, weapon leveled to finish him off once and for all.

"See that, Jack? In the movies you never get to break a cute little tyke's arm. Just can't happen. Here, happens every day. See Jack, *bad guys win.*"

Slater looked down the barrel, unflinching. Ready to die. Behind the wall, Danny sobbed uncontrollably. Except not really. There were no tears in his eyes. Danny had learned well from Whitney. Fake fear. Fake panic. Wait for your chance to strike.

And this was Danny's chance. He had blown it with the punk who broke into his apartment; he had been too frightened to fight back at school. But that was the past. This time, things would be different.

Danny was watching Benedict closely, his eyes boring into the bad guy's back. It was time to attack. Danny broadsided Benedict with everything he had, hitting him like a preteen locomotive and sending him flying. Benedict came down close to Slater. Jack rolled and grabbed him by the throat, throwing him back.

Benedict tottered to his feet, off-balance at the edge of the building. Danny had his gun, and he threw it.

"Jack! Catch!"

Slater's fist closed around the grip, and he raised the weapon, targeting Benedict's explosive black eye.

"No sequel for you," he said and fired.

The bullet burst into the bomb. One moment Benedict was there, the next he was gone, replaced by a great tower of explosive fire shooting skyward. The entire corner of the building was blown to smithereens along with Benedict, and suddenly the sky was full of debris, mixing with the cold rain and floating to the ground.

Slater fell back, exhausted, pain pounding through his body. "There," he said, "there's your damn explosion."

"We gotta get you help!"

Wafting on the breeze like an autumn leaf was a small, smoldering, slightly charred piece of paper. The ticket, glowing with power even now, drifted on the wind, spiraling slowly, ever downwards, to the bright streets. It hit the sidewalk and skipped a few yards, caught in a whirling column of air in front of a movie house.

On the marquee: TONIGHT ONLY—THE SEVENTH SEAL

Inside the theater Death, the Grim Reaper himself, was playing chess. But Death seemed to have lost interest in the game. He raised his hooded head, like a watchdog, and then stood up and walked off the screen, out of the movie, down the aisle and out the front door of the theater.

Mrs. Madigan, one of the few art movie fans watching the film in the cavernous theater, did what anyone would do if Death suddenly walked out of a movie. She joined the stampede for the exits.

TWENTY-FIVE

The ambulance careened through the crowded, wet streets, the siren screaming. Danny was seated next to the driver, his head thrust into the rear of the vehicle, watching as the emergency medical technicians worked on Slater's shattered body.

"Shortness of breath."

One of the technicians pressed a stethoscope to Slater's chest. "Diaphretic. His lung has collapsed." The man's voice was flat and unemotional.

One of the monitoring devices patched to Slater's body began to beep ominously. "Fluid challenge," said the first technician. "Do a bilateral IV. Full open."

The medics were all business—this wasn't Jack Slater, movie star. This was just another gunshot victim on a rainy Manhattan night. Jack's head lolled to one side, and what Danny saw in those eyes cut into him like a sharp knife. There was a faraway sadness on Jack Slater's face. He was a wounded animal now, lost in civilization, cut off from his native forest, confused and betrayed by his surroundings.

The monitor was beeping faster, more urgently. The medics exchanged grim looks. One gave a thumbs-down. "Think we're losing this one . . ."

"You can't save him?" stammered Danny.

The medic wouldn't look at him. "We're doing all we can do, kid."

"It isn't enough," said Danny intently. "He needs to get back home. Back where it's just a flesh wound, back where he does ten sequels."

The EMS guys looked at him as if he was crazy. "What the hell are you talking about?"

"Don't you understand?" beseeched Danny, "*We've got to take him to the movies!*"

"The movies?"

Danny did what he had to do. He pulled Benedict's revolver from his jacket pocket and waved it at the driver. "Turn around. We gotta go back.

The driver never hesitated. He stood on the brakes, and the ambulance lurched to a halt. In a flash, he threw open the door of the cab and started running. "Hey! Get back here. You can't just take off like that."

He turned and looked into the back of the ambulance just in time to see the medics dashing out the rear of the vehicle. "Great. Just great! They always run away!"

Danny slid behind the wheel and breathed deeply. "Hang on, Jack," he yelled and hit the gas. The ambulance lurched forward, slithering into the clumsiest U-turn in New York traffic history, then roaring back up Eighth Avenue.

Slater managed to lift himself off the gurney. "Do you know how to drive?"

"Sure," Danny screamed over the siren. "I watched *you* do it, didn't I?"

Danny threw the ambulance into a tight turn on Forty-Second Street, heading east. Then, in front of the Pandora, he wrenched the wheel to the right, barreling across three lanes of traffic and straight into the lobby of the theater, taking out the double doors in a shower of glass.

Danny was running on pure adrenaline now, as he piloted the ambulance across the lobby and straight down the center aisle of the theater. Screeching to halt in the middle of the sea of seats, he threw open the rear door and hauled Jack out.

"Nick! Nick! Fire up the projector! Slater's dying!"

Nick's face appeared in the peephole of the projection booth, high up above the balcony.

"You got the ticket?" he yelled.

"No. But it's gotta work." He was hustling Slater toward the screen. "It's gotta!"

Nick got busy, and a moment later, the bright white light of the projectors flooded the giant screen. Danny fell against the screen, feeling frantically for the way back into the movie world. Slater had sunk to his knees and was watching his friend with hollow eyes.

Danny pounded the screen with his fists. "It won't open, Jack—we need the ticket stub. It won't open!"

Slater nodded and rested his head on the floor. "That's okay, kid. No sweat. You tried . . ." He coughed and sighed, the life fading from him.

Danny dropped to his knees and seized Jack Slater's head, cradling it. "Jack . . . Please, Jack . . . Please don't die . . ."

And then the shadow of death fell over them. Literally. Standing in the bright light, as if blotting out hope itself, was the figure of the Grim Reaper in person.

Danny looked up, but didn't hesitate. He whipped the gun from his belt. "Back off," he snarled. "You can't have him. I've had it up to here with you, mister—who stays, who goes— well, I'm telling you. *This one stays!*"

Not surprisingly, Death spoke with the deep, cold voice of doom. It was *what* he said that shocked Danny. "I was only curious." He pointed a bony finger at Jack Slater. "He is not on any of my lists." Death paused for a moment. "Though *you* are, Daniel."

Daniel figured he had heard just about everything. "*Now?*"

Death shook his head. "Oh no . . . You'll die a grandfather." The Grim Reaper turned and started to walk up the aisle.

Danny sprung after him. "Hey! Wait a minute! Help us! You've gotta get him back. You can do it. I know you can!"

Death shook his head slowly. "I don't do fiction. Not my field. Sorry. You're a very brave young man. Someone must have taught you well . . ." Death paused for a long moment. "However, unfortunately, it seems as if you're not very bright. If I were you, I'd be looking for the other half of the ticket."

Danny blinked, twice, very rapidly. Thinking hard. Then he punched the air. "Yessss!"

And he was off, running up the aisle, throwing a body block on Nick's old ticket barrel, sending the container flying, tickets scattering on the floor like confetti. Danny scrambled among the tickets and found it—but it wasn't glowing.

Danny raced back to Slater, slapping the ticket, waving it like a banner, yelling at it in an attempt to get the damn thing to come to life. He skidded to halt next to Slater, showing him the ticket as if it were a sacred relic.

"I've got it, Jack—I'll get you home, you'll see. You can't die."

Almost all the strength had drained from Jack's body. It was all he could do to smile and gasp a few words. "I know . . . not till the grosses go down . . ."

Danny held up the ticket. "This is gonna save us."

Slater stretched out his hand dismissively. "Throw that silly thing away." But the instant he touched the piece of paper, the ticket began to glow. A triumphant scream broke from Danny's lips, and suddenly the white light on the screen began to change, iridescent color flooding from the projectors, filling the screen with an image, indistinct at first, hazy and hard to make out. But as the cameras focused and pulled back, a giant brown eye flashed on the screen. It was Lieutenant Dekker's eye, filled with the rage that Danny Madigan knew and loved.

Dekker was pacing his office. "Dammit! Where's Slater?!"

Suddenly, they were in the movie—Jack and Danny were back where *anything* was possible. Jack was still hurt, and he was sprawled on the floor of the detective's squad room.

"Help!" Danny yelled. "Somebody!"

The Animated Cat bounded into view and stared at Slater. "Oh no! They got Jack!"

"Get a doctor!" Danny ordered.

Slater thrust the ticket back into Danny's hand. "Hurry. You've got to get back."

Danny shook his head. "No! I'm not going to leave you!"

"Danny," Jack pleaded. "I'm just an imaginary action hero. You've got a real life."

"You're real to me," he said fervently. "Don't you see? You're the best thing in . . . I need you to . . ."

Slater filled in the words for him. "To be here where you can always find me. And I need you to be out there to believe in me . . . and to take care of your mother for me because—"

"My mother? Because why?"

"Never mind. Look—you've got your whole life ahead of you. That should be enough."

Danny nodded. "And pimples and premature ejaculation, I heard." But there was something else on Danny's mind, something he couldn't quite bring himself to say.

"What? What is it?"

"I'm just afraid you'll forget me," he said, feeling like a wimp. But it was the painful truth, nonetheless.

Slater smiled. "Anyone who thinks that would be making . . . *a big mistake*."

Danny could only grin. A moment later, the animated cat led a horde of cops into the room, and they swarmed around Slater, shunting Danny aside. He backed away and, with a wink from Slater, slipped back through the movie screen and into real life. Danny walked backward up the aisle, watching the action on the screen unfold.

"Outta my way! You want a doctor? I'm a doctor." The doctor knelt down next to Slater and pushed away the tatters of his T-shirt. The examination was cursory to say the least. "Is this a joke?" the doctor demanded. "I wouldn't even call this a flesh wound! Whiskers, just wash him up good. He'll be fine."

"Thanks, Doc," said the animated cat.

Danny grinned and sighed. What was a life-threatening injury in the real world was nothing more than a scratch in the land of the movies. Everything was back in its proper place; the earth was ordered and logical again.

There was a fast change of scene on the screen. The door to Dekker's office came flying off its hinges, and Jack Slater pounded into the room. His clothes were fresh, his cigar brand new. There wasn't a scratch on him.

"You wanted to see me, Lieutenant?"

"Damn right I did," Dekker yelled. "Where the hell have you been? The cost of the door is coming out of your meager but totally undeserved paycheck, Slater." Then, for no real reason, except for the fact that it was his movie idiom, he added: "I've got the Save the Eagle Foundation doing the funky tango up and down my Hershey Highway—" He yanked open the wide middle drawer and dumped all of Slater's weaponry and his badge on the top of the desk. "Now, take this stuff and hit the streets."

Slater leaned in, getting right in Dekker's face. "Make believe you have a brain, 'cause I'm only saying this once: starting today, I want twice my salary and extra for every virgin I save. I want a CD player, the works of Mozart and an apartment—*not near the freeway*—with *a terrace I can plant flowers on. And I want a real bed. King-sized.*" *Jack turned and faced the camera and shot an enormous wink at Danny.*

"Mozart!?" screamed Dekker, in stunned disbelief.

Danny and Nick were watching together now, standing in the middle of the theater.

And Slater wasn't finished yet. "And furthermore, what's all this garbage with guns? There's ninety thousand kids with guns out there as it is. Why don't we have other things, like programs? I don't want to be taking lives, I wanna be enriching them. Without some Hollywood genius dictating my every move. Got it?"

"Got it," said Dekker sourly.

Danny and Nick were heading for the exit. "You got to be a magician after all, Nick, the ticket really does work. Here . . ." Danny tried to hand the ticket back to Nick, its rightful owner, but the old man shook his head slowly.

"No, the ticket is yours, Danny. And I think maybe the magic was too. Keep it."

Danny's eyes glowed, and he slipped the scrap of paper into the back pocket of his blue jeans. Nick draped his arm across Danny's shoulder as they headed for the door.

Coming toward them was Irene Madigan, fear and worry writ large on her face.

"Danny!"

"Mom!" Danny threw himself into her arms, and she hugged him close.

"I'm not going to ask you what happened. I'm not going to ask where you've been. Maybe on my deathbed, you'll tell me everything and it'll all sound perfectly reasonable. Oh God, Danny, I thought I had lost you too."

Danny comforted his mother, sounding older than his years. "It's okay, Ma. Everything's okay now. I took care of it."

Danny's mother smiled. "You took care of what? The future of the world?" She pulled back and looked at him. "Maybe even the future of Danny Madigan?"

Danny smiled. "Maybe."

Arm in arm, they walked toward the exit. "So . . . um," said Mrs. Madigan casually. "So where's Jack?"

"Oh. He had to go back to LA."

Irene's face fell. "Oh."

Danny peered at her questioningly. "Why?"

Mrs. Madigan shook her head, as if it were nothing. "I just thought maybe the three of us might have dinner . . . Y'know . . . once in a while. Maybe take in a movie."

Danny's smile broadened, and he slipped his hand into his back pocket. "I think I got a way to arrange it." He gave his mother a huge wink. "Y'know. Once in a while."